MARY ANNE'S
BAD-LUCK MYSTERY

Ann M. Martin

Hippo Books
Scholastic Publications Limited
London

Scholastic Children's Books,
Scholastic Publications Ltd.,
7-9 Pratt Street, London NW1 0AE, UK

Scholastic Inc.,
730 Broadway, New York, NY 10003, USA

Scholastic Canada Ltd.,
123 Newkirk Road, Richmond Hill,
Ontario Canada, L4C 3G5

Ashton Scholastic Pty. Ltd.,
P O Box 579, Gosford, New South Wales,
Australia

Ashton Scholastic Ltd.,
Private Bag 1, Penrose, Auckland,
New Zealand

First published by Scholastic Inc., USA, 1988
Published in the UK by Scholastic Publications Ltd, 1991

Text copyright © Ann M. Martin, 1988

ISBN 0 590 76474 8

THE BABY-SITTERS CLUB is a trademark of Scholastic Inc.

Printed by Cox & Wyman Ltd, Reading, Berks.
Typeset in Plantin by AKM Associates (UK) Ltd., Southall, London

10 9 8 7 6 5 4 3 2 1

1st CHAPTER

"You know," said Kristy Thomas, "I've been thinking. If I took a bunch of these old wilted peas and put them in the mashed potatoes—evenly spread out—and then took my fork and smushed them all down, my lunch would look almost exactly like—"

"Stop!" I cried. "Stop right there. I don't want to know what you think it would look like."

"Do you want to know what I think it would smell like?" Kristy asked.

"Absolutely not," I replied, turning green. "Please. Don't say another word about the lunch. Why do you buy the hot lunch every day, anyway? Why don't you buy a salad or something?"

"Because," replied Kristy, "it's so much more fun to say disgusting things about the hot lunch."

Everyone laughed. We couldn't help it.

1

'We' were five of the members of the Babysitters Club—Kristy, me (Mary Anne Spier), my friends Dawn Shafer and Claudia Kishi, and Logan Bruno. (I guess you would call Logan my boyfriend.) It was a Monday and it was eighth-grade lunchtime at Stoneybrook Middle School. That meant we were sitting around our usual table. In front of Kristy and Logan and me were hot lunches; in front of Claudia was a tunafish sandwich; and in front of Dawn, the health-food nut, was a lunch from home—an apple, some cottage cheese, a plastic container of this brown-rice casserole, and something Dawn called trail mix, which really looked more like birdseed.

Dawn is from California, which explains a lot.

"Just out of curiosity," spoke up Logan, "what *would* the peas and mashed potatoes look like, Kristy?"

"Oh, please! Oh, please! Don't egg her on," I exclaimed. "Logan, why are you doing this to me?"

"It's fun watching you turn green," Logan replied.

The five of us began to laugh again. We really are great friends. And we always sit together. Well, at any rate, us girls always sit together. Logan only sits with us about half the time. The rest of the time, he sits with his other friends. Understandably, those other friends are boys. If you were a thirteen-year-old guy, do you think you could sit with a table full of girls every lunch break?

No.

Kristy is my oldest friend in the world. She used to live next door to me. In fact, we lived next door to each other all our lives— until last summer. Last summer, Kristy's mum, who was divorced, got remarried. The man she married lives in a gigantic house, a mansion really, on the other side of our town, which is Stoneybrook, Connecticut. So Kristy and her mum and her three brothers (Sam and Charlie, who are in high school, and David Michael, who's just seven) moved into Watson Brewer's house. Now Kristy also has a little stepbrother, Andrew, who's four, and a little stepsister, Karen, who's six. (They live with Kristy's family every other weekend. The rest of the time they live with their mother and stepfather.)

I miss Kristy a lot, even though a very nice family moved into *her* house, and even though I've become really close to Dawn. Dawn moved to Connecticut from California last January, about ten months ago. She and I hit it off right away, and now she and Kristy are both my best friends, even though they are very different people. Here's a comparison of the three of us:

Kristy is outspoken. "Big Mouth" might be a better way to describe her. She's sort of

3

a tomboy, is full of ideas, and acts like a blender on high speed. By that I mean she's going, going, going all the time. Sometimes I just want to say to her, "Give it a rest, Kristy!" Kristy doesn't care much about how she looks (she *always* wears jeans, a sweater if necessary, and trainers), and she is not interested in boys. In fact, she doesn't like most of them. (Logan is an exception.) Kristy basically thinks that boys are like flies—pests. That's because she's been unfortunate enough to know mostly the annoying ones. Kristy likes sports and children and is the founder and chairman of the Babysitters Club, which I'll tell you more about later. She has brown hair and brown eyes. She and I are the two shortest girls in the entire eighth grade.

Dawn is, well, she's *Dawn*. She's this California girl who's trying to get adjusted to life on the East Coast—to cold weather and to people who'd rather eat a beefburger than soybeans. Like Kristy, she's also adjusting to some changes in her family. The reason she moved here was that her parents got divorced. Her mother had grown up in Stoneybrook, so she brought Dawn and her younger brother, Jeff, back to her hometown. Only it didn't exactly work out. Jeff was really unhappy, and finally, a few weeks ago, went back to California to live with his dad, so now it's just Dawn and her mother. (They're very

close.) Unlike Kristy, Dawn does care about how she looks—and she's pretty good-looking. She has waist-length hair the colour of wheat. Actually, it's almost white. And piercing blue eyes. And she wears trendy clothes, but she's very individualistic about it. In fact, she's just generally an individual. Dawn does things her way and doesn't care what other people think. She isn't snobby, she's just very sure of herself.

Now I, on the other hand, am not self-assured like Dawn, and I'm not outspoken like Kristy. I'm quiet and shy. So why am I the only one of my friends with a steady boyfriend? I don't know. Maybe it's because I'm sensitive. People are always telling me I'm sensitive. When I was younger they meant it as *too* sensitive—in other words, a baby. Now they mean it as caring and understanding. I must say that when my friends are upset or having problems, they come to me quite often. They don't always come for advice. Sometimes they just come to talk, because they know I'll listen. Like Kristy, I don't care too much about the clothes I wear, although lately I'm taking more of an interest. It's fun to dress in baggy sweaters or short dresses, or to put on bright jewellery or hair clips or something. (I used to go to school in boring old dresses and shoes.) Like Dawn, I live with just one parent—my dad. My mum died when I was really little, and I don't have any brothers or

5

sisters. I do have a pet, though. He's my grey kitten named Tigger. I don't know what I'd do without him.

So, that's Dawn and Kristy and me. Now let me tell you about Claudia and Logan. Talk about people being different, wait until you hear about Claudia. Claudia Kishi is the most exotic, interesting person in the eighth grade. Honest. First of all, she's Japanese-American and has this long, silky, jet-black hair, these dark eyes, and a perfect complexion. Then there's the matter of her clothes. Nobody, but nobody, dresses like Claudia. At least, nobody in our year. (We used to have a friend, another member of the Babysitters Club, named Stacey McGill, who dressed kind of like Claudia. But Stacey moved back to New York, where she used to live. And anyway, trust me, Claudia is unique.) The best way to get this point across is to describe to you what Claudia was wearing at lunch that day. It was her vegetable blouse, an oversized white shirt with a green vegetable print all over it— cabbages and courgettes and turnips and stuff. Under the blouse was a *very* short denim skirt, white tights, green ankle socks over the tights, and lavender trainers, the kind boys usually wear, with a lot of rubber and big laces and the name of the manufacturer in huge letters on the sides. Wait, I've not finished. Claudia had pulled the hair on one side of her head back with a yellow clip that looked like a poodle. The hair on the other side of her head was hanging in her face. Attached to the one ear you could see was a plastic earring about the size of a jar lid.

Awesome!

Some more things about Claudia: She is not a good student. She loves art and mysteries. She's addicted to junk food.

On to Logan. It's a little hard to describe him because I like him so much. Do you know what I mean? I mean that I think everything about him is incredible and handsome and wonderful, and that probably isn't entirely true. So I'll have to try hard to be realistic. In terms of looks, Logan is perfect. Well, maybe not perfect. Maybe more like unbelievable. No. Let's just say he has blondish-brown hair . . . and he looks exactly like Cam Geary, the most gorgeous boy TV star I can think of. In terms of personality he's understanding and funny and likes kids, which means a lot to me. Logan used to live in Kentucky, so he has this interesting southern accent. For instance, he pronounces my name "May-rih Ay-on Speeyuh." And he says "Ahm" instead of "I'm" and "Luevulle" instead of "Louisville" (which is the city he lived in). It is simply too hard to describe Logan anymore. Really, all you need to know is that we understand each other completely, and we like each other a *lot*.

"So," Claudia said, after we'd stopped looking at Kristy's disgusting lunch tray, "who's going to the Halloween Hop?"

The Hallo*ween* Hop?" said Kristy disdainfully. "Is it time for *that* again?"

"Halloween is coming up soon," Dawn pointed out.

"I really love this time of year," Claudia said dreamily.

"Why?" asked Kristy. "*You* get dressed up every day."

"Ha, ha," said Claudia.

"Oh, come on. I'm only teasing."

(Kristy's mouth gets her in trouble a lot.)

"Well," I said, hoping to calm Claudia down, "Logan and I are going to the Hop."

"In costume?" Dawn wanted to know.

Logan and I looked at each other and shrugged. "We can't decide," I told my friends. It might be fun to get dressed up, but sometimes you can feel pretty silly. Especially if a lot of kids don't wear costumes.

It was right then that I got the creepy feeling that someone was staring at me. You know? When the skin on the back of your neck begins to crawl? It's as if you can feel each individual hair back there.

It is not a pleasant feeling.

Was I spooked because we were talking about Halloween, or was someone really staring at me?

Very slowly I looked over my left shoulder.

8

Two tables away, Grace Blume, Cokie Mason, and two other girls were pointing in our direction and snickering. It was hard to tell who they were pointing at, but I think it was Kristy. Probably because she was wearing the same clothes she'd been wearing for the last seven weeks.

Or was it me? Quickly, I checked to see if there was mashed potato on the end of my nose, or if my sweater was on backward or something. I looked okay . . . didn't I? This is what I mean about not being self-assured like Dawn. At the slightest sign of trouble, I assume that whatever is going wrong has something to do with me, or is my fault.

I glanced back over at Grace and Cokie. (Just in case you care, Cokie's real name is Marguerite. Who knows where "Cokie" came from.) Grace and Cokie and their friends were still staring at us.

I heard Grace say something about "stuck up". Okay, so I know some people think our club is snobby because we sit together all the time. At least, we had done lately. Last year, Kristy and I used to sit with other friends—the Shillaber twins, mostly. And Stacey (who was still in Stoneybrook then) and Claudia used to sit with a big group of kids, boys and girls—Rick Chow, Dorianne Wallingford, and Pete Black, to name a few. (Dawn, being an individual, would go back and forth between our group and the other one.)

9

If you want my honest opinion, I think there are some hurt feelings this year. The people we used to spend time with feel left out because the Babysitters Club is our new group. I feel kind of bad about that, but I don't know what to do. I guess the twins and Rick and Dorianne and everyone will have to be their own groups.

"Hey," Kristy whispered. (We all leaned over to hear her better.) "If Cokie took a picture of Logan it would last longer. Right now she's boring holes in the back of his head with her eyes."

"That does it," said Logan. "I'm going to the boys' table. I'm tired of being teased for sitting with you guys."

"You mean with us *girls*," I corrected him. I understood Logan well enough to know that he wasn't mad, just annoyed. Sometimes he does take flak for being the only boy in the Babysitters Club.

"Too late," Kristy announced as the bell rang, signalling the end of lunch. "You can abandon us tomorrow, Logan."

Logan grinned.

We all got to our feet.

"Hey, don't forget," Kristy said as we began to scatter. "Club meeting today. See you at five-thirty!"

2nd
CHAPTER

I just love checking our mailbox. There is something about getting mail that is exciting. Going out to the box each afternoon is sometimes the highlight of my day. You never know what will be in it. There could be anything—letters (they're best, of course, but only when they're addressed to me), catalogues, coupons, the *Stoneybrook News* (I like to read about crime—burglaries and mysteries and stuff), and interesting magazines. Plus, around holidays and your birthday, you can start watching for parcels and greetings cards.

The only problem with our mail is that it isn't delivered until about five o'clock in the afternoon. That's all right on a school day, but during the summer you could die waiting for that blue-and-white van to come down the street.

Anyway, on the afternoon of the day that

Kristy was being do disgusting about her lunch, I baby-sat for this little kid named Jimmy Newton until almost five-thirty. Then I rushed over to Claudia's for our meeting of the Babysitters Club. But on the way, I just couldn't resist a quick peek in our mailbox.

When I opened it, it was stuffed! Just the way I like it. I sorted through bills (boring), some ads (kind of interesting), two magazines (yea!), and then I saw it—a letter addressed to me! Oh, wow! I was ecstatic.

Since it was five-thirty by then, I grabbed the letter, stuck it in my pocket, shoved everything else back in the box, and ran across the street to Claudia's. I didn't want to be late for the meeting.

Maybe now would be a good time for me to tell you just what the Babysitters Club is. Well, as I mentioned earlier, it was Kristy's idea and she started it. She got the idea a little over a year ago (when she still lived next door to me), after she noticed how hard it was for her mum to get a sitter for David Michael if Kristy wasn't available. Sometimes Mrs Thomas would have to make four or five calls before she found a person who was free. So Kristy thought there must be other parents around here with the same problem. Then she thought how terrific it would be if a parent could make just one phone call and reach several sitters at the same time. So she got together with Claudia,

Stacey, and me since we all did a lot of baby-sitting, and we formed the club.

Here's how the club works. Every Monday, Wednesday, and Friday afternoon from five-thirty until six o'clock, the members gather in Claudia's bedroom. Claudia has her own private phone and private phone number, and parents call us at Claudia's when they need to line up a sitter. There are six of us in the club now, plus two associate members (I'll explain all that later), so our clients are bound to wind up with a sitter. With eight of us, somebody is always free.

How do our clients know when and where to reach us? Because we advertise, that's how. Kristy's busy brain is always clicking along, thinking of important stuff like advertisements. That's one reason she's club chairman. (Also, the club was her idea, so who would you expect to be chairman?)

Claudia is the vice-chairman. We felt that was only fair, since we were going to be meeting in her room and using her phone.

I'm the secretary. I suspect that this is mostly because of my neat handwriting, but I would like to think that it's also because I'm organized and can manage things well. As secretary, it's my job to keep our club record book up to date. The record book is where we keep track of our job appointments, our clients, and their names and addresses and stuff.

Dawn is our treasurer. That used to be

Stacey McGill's job, but when she moved back to New York, Dawn took over. (Dawn had joined the club several months after it started, and she became our alternate officer. She could take over the job of anyone who couldn't make a meeting, sort of like a substitute teacher.) Anyway, as treasurer, it's up to her to keep a record of the money we earn, and to collect club subs and see that our treasury doesn't get too low. We use the treasury money to pay Charlie to drive Kristy to and from the meetings, since she now lives too far away to walk; to buy food for club parties; and to replace the stuff in our Kid-Kits. (Kristy invented Kid-Kits. They're boxes that we sometimes take along when we baby-sit. We keep them filled with our old games and toys, plus new colouring books and crayons and things. Kids love them, and their parents love *us* for bringing them!)

Now, I said before that the club has six members plus two associate members. Logan is one of the associate members. The other is a girl named Shannon Kilbourne, who lives across the street from Kristy in Kristy's fancy new neighbourhood. The associate members don't come to the meetings; they're people we can call on in a pinch—when none of the regular club members is free to take a job. This way, we never have to disappoint a client.

The two *other* girls in the club are junior

14

members. They're eleven years old and in the sixth grade, so they're only allowed to sit after school and on weekends, not at night (unless they're taking care of their own brothers and sisters). Their names are Mallory Pike and Jessica Ramsey, and they joined the club quite recently, right after Stacey left, as a matter of fact. I really like both Mal and Jessi, even if they are a little young. What's important is that they're good, responsible baby-sitters, and furthermore, they're just plain *nice*.

Mallory used to be someone our club sat *for*. She's the oldest of eight children, so she knows a lot about taking care of kids. Mal is going through sort of an awkward stage. She has freckles and curly hair, neither of which Mrs Pike will let her do anything about. She wants pierced ears but isn't allowed to have them yet; wants contact lenses but isn't allowed to have *them* yet, either; and doesn't want braces for her teeth but is getting them, anyway. Mal loves to read and write and draw, and she might become an author when she grows up.

Like Kristy and me, Jessi and Mal are best friends who are alike in a lot of ways and different in a lot of ways. They're alike in that it's just plain awful to be eleven. Jessi also wants pierced ears but isn't allowed to get them yet, and is facing a mouthful of metal. And she also loves to read, especially horse stories. She's not a writer, though.

15

Instead, she's a *very* talented ballet dancer. (As well as a good joke-teller.) Jessi has a younger sister, Becca, and a baby brother, Squirt. The Ramseys moved to Stoneybrook very recently. (In fact, they moved into Stacey's house after the McGills moved out of it.) And, boy, did they have a tough time at first. The Ramseys are black, and there aren't many black families around here at all, and none in Jessi's neighbourhood. Jessi is the only black kid in the sixth grade, if you can believe it. However, things are settling down and getting easier for her family. I think the Babysitters Club is important to Jessi because it gives her a feeling of belonging.

Before I tell you about the memorable meeting we had that day, there's just one other thing you need to know about the running of our club: the club notebook. This is a sort of diary that Kristy makes us keep, which no one likes writing in except Mallory, and maybe Kristy. In it, we describe every single baby-sitting job we go on—which kids we sit for and what goes on. Once a week we're supposed to read the past week's entries so that we all know what's happening with our clients. I have to admit, it's pretty helpful, even if writing in it can be a great big bore.

All right. Back to the meeting.

I rushed to Claudia's front door with the letter tucked in my pocket. I rang the bell but went right on inside. I've lived across the street from Claudia forever, so it's okay to do that.

"Hi, Mimi!" I called to Claudia's grand-mother as I ran upstairs. Ordinarily, I would have stopped to talk to her, but I was on the late side that day, and Kristy likes us members to be on time.

When I reached Claudia's room, I saw that I wasn't the last person to arrive. Jessi was still missing. She's usually late because after school she either goes to her ballet class, which is all the way over in Stamford, or goes to her steady sitting job for this family, the Braddocks.

I joined Claudia and Dawn, who were draped across Claudia's bed, looking through our seventh-grade yearbook. The six of us almost always sit in the same places during meetings. Claudia, Dawn, and me on the bed; Jessi and Mal on the floor, and Kristy in the director's chair.

Get this. Our chairman holds meetings with a pencil stuck over one ear, wearing a visor. She says she feels more official that way. I haven't mentioned this to her, but I've never seen the President of the United States sitting in a director's chair, wearing a visor.

As I was settling down on the bed, Jessi ran into the room.

"Good. We're all here," said Kristy. "Let's begin."

Darn. I was just about to open my letter.

I didn't get a chance to do that until about fifteen minutes later, when we hit a lull. All official business had been conducted and the phone wasn't ringing, for a change.

I pulled the letter out of my pocket and tore it open.

"What's that?" asked Kristy.

"I got a letter today!" I said. "But I don't know who it's from. There's no return address."

I unfolded the paper that had been in the envelope.

"Oh, darn!" I exclaimed. "Darn, darn, boring *darn*."

"What?" asked Mallory.

"It's a dumb old chain letter, that's what. I *hate* chain letters. You have to send them to everyone you know, and then *they* have to send them to everyone *they* know."

"What kind of chain letter is it?" Dawn asked. "The kind where you send a postcard to the name at the top of the list and a few weeks later you supposedly get a million cards yourself?"

"I don't think so," I replied. "There's no list of names on this letter."

I read the letter quickly. I began to feel chills. Then I read the letter again, more slowly. When I finished, I was covered with goose bumps.

"This is really weird," I told my friends. "With this letter, you don't get anything for not breaking the chain—except good luck. But if you *do* break the chain, the letter says, 'Bad luck will be visited upon you, the recipient of this letter, and your friends and loved ones. Harm will come your way.'"

"Yikes," said Mal.

"Ho-hum," said Kristy.

"I wish I knew who sent it," I mused.

"Do you recognize the handwriting?" asked Claudia.

"There's no handwriting. The letter's typed." I looked at the envelope. "So's the address."

"Oh, well," said Kristy. "That stuff's just stupid, anyway. Who believes in causing bad luck by not mailing out a bunch of letters? How many are you supposed to send anyway, Mary Anne?"

"Twenty," I said.

"Well, don't bother sending one to me. I'll just break the chain.

"Don't worry," I told Kristy. "I'm not going to send *any*. Everyone would hate me because then they'd have to send out twenty letters, and besides, I don't think I even *know* twenty people."

"What?" screeched Mallory. During all this, Mal and Jessi had been staring at me, terrified. "You mean you're going to break the chain? That's crazy! Thanks a lot!"

"Yeah!" exclaimed Jessi. "If *you* break it, bad luck will be visited upon *us*, our friends, and loved ones."

"Oh, it will not," said Claudia. "At least, I don't think so. Do you, Dawn?"

"Of course not . . . I mean, I guess not."

"Well, do you want me to send letters to you?" I asked Claudia and Dawn.

They looked at each other. Finally Dawn said, "We want you to send the letters—but not to us."

I giggled. "See? You don't want to have to deal with them. And neither do I. You know how much it costs to use the Xerox at the library? Fifteen cents a page. I'd have to have, um, let's see . . . well, a lot of change. Plus twenty stamps, plus twenty envelopes. And what would I wind up with? Twenty enemies."

"I wouldn't mind getting the letter, Mary Anne," said Mallory.

"Me neither," said Jessi nervously.

"Oh, you guys," Kristy admonished them. "It's just superstition. Forget it. But if you're so worried, why don't you take care of Mary Anne's letter for her?"

"It doesn't work that way," Mallory replied. "The letter was addressed to Mary Anne. She's the one who has to answer it.

"Well, anyway," I said. "Kristy's right. This is just superstition. I think."

I wasn't positive about that, but I was pretty sure. In fact, I was so sure that when the meeting was over, I tossed the letter in Claudia's wastebasket as I left the room.

3rd CHAPTER

I may be clumsy sometimes, but I swear, I haven't fallen out of bed since I was four years old. However, that was exactly how I began the next day.

It was 6:45. I was dreaming about climbing a mountain (I haven't been mountain climbing in my entire life), the alarm clock rang, and I fell off the mountain.

How embarrassing.

What was even more embarrassing was that my father heard the crash and rushed into my room. He found me on the floor, tangled up in the blankets. Plus, I scared Tigger. He slunk underneath my desk and wouldn't come out.

"Mary Anne?" said my dad. "Are you all right?"

A reasonable question.

"Yeah," I replied, shaking my head and wishing for the floor to swallow me up. Or at

21

the very least, wishing to die, which would put an end to the embarrassment.

I stood up. "I was having this dream," I tried to explain. "I was climbing a mountain, and then the alarm rang—"

"And you fell off the mountain?" asked Dad.

"Yes! How did you know?"

"I've had some strange dreams myself," he replied. "Okay now?"

"Fine. Just embarrassed," I admitted.

Dad smiled. "You get dressed. I'll make pancakes for breakfast."

"Oh, super!" I exclaimed.

My dad used to be this incredibly strict, stiff person. He had all sorts of rules for me, like I had to wear my hair in plaits, and he had to approve of the outfits I chose for school, and I couldn't ride my bike downtown with friends. But then we started the Babysitters Club, and I found out some important things about myself. Mostly, I found out that I was much more grown-up and responsible than Dad thought I was. When I proved that to him, he started to change. He relaxed his rules, he relaxed around me, he relaxed in general. Things are *so* different than they were a year ago.

Don't get me wrong. I'm not blaming Dad for the way he used to be. Remember, he's raising me alone. He has to be both mother and father, and I think that before, he was just trying too hard.

We are both much happier.

Dad left to start breakfast. He closed my door behind him.

"Tigger, Tigger," I called. I got down on my hands and knees and peered under the desk. "Come on out, Tigger, you 'fraidy cat," I said. "It's safe. There's nothing to be scared of."

Tigger began to creep out. I could see his yellow eyes moving toward me.

"Good boy," I said. But as I straightened up, I banged into the chair.

CRASH.

Tigger dived back under the desk.

"I'm sorry, I'm sorry," I told him. Too late. I knew he'd stay there until he was so hungry he would have to come out for his breakfast.

I opened my wardrobe and managed to get dressed without killing myself. Except for my shoes. I couldn't find them. I looked everywhere. They were the same shoes I'd worn yesterday. Since I hadn't come home from school barefoot, I knew they were around somewhere. Oh, well. I could search for them later.

I made my bed, washed my face, called to Tigger again, and ran downstairs. Dad had breakfast waiting. He's an early riser, and he actually *likes* to rush around and get things done before seven-thirty in the morning.

"Mmmm," I said, as I slid into my chair. "Pancakes *and* bacon!"

I reached for my orange juice and knocked over the glass. Juice ran across the table. Dad was standing by the fridge, so he was safe, but the juice cascaded into my lap.

I was wearing a white dress.

"Oh, *no!*" I cried, leaping to my feet. "Dad, I'm sorry! Really I am. I know you said a white dress wasn't practical for school, but I've worn it five times and nothing happened to it be—"

"Mary Anne, it's *all right*," Dad told me. He handed me some paper towels. "Here, Mop up. The fill a basin with cold water and soak your dress in it. Just leave it there. I'll keep your breakfast warm in the oven while you change your clothes . . . and find your shoes."

Boy, some morning I was having.

I changed my clothes and ate my breakfast. Then I looked for my shoes. I found them on top of the TV set. I had no idea why they were there. I didn't stop to wonder, though. If I didn't leave right then, I'd miss walking to school with Claudia.

So I put my shoes on and ran out the door. Claudia was standing around on the pavement in front of the house.

"Hi," she greeted me. "What were you doing?"

"Looking for my shoes, changing my clothes, and comforting Tigger," I replied. I told her about the morning I was having.

I made a big deal out of it, hoping that,

magically, this would put an end to things. You know how when you have a complaint about something—like a teacher who's being mean to you, or the rubber bands on your braces that keep snapping—and you finally tell someone about it, then that's the end of the problem? Well, I was sort of hoping that would happen with my bad day. That if I complained to Claudia, not a single other thing would go wrong.

It didn't work.

We reached school okay, but when I got there, I couldn't open my locker. Finally, I had to find Mr Halprin, the caretaker, and ask him to do it for me.

In maths class I realized I'd left my homework right where I'd done it: at home.

In the dining room I spilled a plate of macaroni and cheese. Not on me, on the floor. Mr Halprin had to come again. We were getting to know each other.

One of the worst things about that day happened right after Mr Halprin left. Logan turned to me and said, "So, is Mr Halprin a close, personal friend of yours?"

Since I'd just been thinking that Mr Halprin and I were sort of getting to know each other, I'm not sure why that remark drove me crazy, but it did. Logan had meant it to be funny. I snapped at him. "Ha. Ha."

"Hey, lighten up," said Logan.

"Easy for you to say," I grumbled.

"Mary *A*-anne." That was Kristy. Our

usual group was crowded around our usual table.

"*Wha*-at?"

"Geez," said Logan, under his breath. "Touchy, touchy."

"Well, how would you feel if you dropped a plate of macaroni and cheese in front of the whole dining room?"

"Not that many people saw," Logan told me quietly.

"Oh, no. Only about three hundred, that's all." And having said that, I got up and stalked off to the school library, where I went looking for *Little Women*. It's one of my favourite books, and I thought that reading some familiar passages might be comforting.

The book was not on the shelf.

I walked home from school by myself that afternoon. I didn't bother to look for any of my friends, but I was sure they wouldn't have wanted to walk with me.

At home, I breathed a sigh of relief. I felt safer somehow, even though home was where I had fallen out of bed, scared Tigger, and knocked over my orange juice. At least I hadn't done those things in front of three hundred kids.

"Oh, Tigger," I said, as I settled myself on my bed with my own copy of *Little Women*. "You stay here with me."

Tigger cuddled up against me, purring like an outboard motor. I opened the book

26

to the scene where Beth dies. Maybe I would feel cheered up if I read about someone who was having a worse time than I was.

That was when the phone rang.

I had to disturb Tigger in order to answer it.

"Hello?" I said.

"Hello, Mary Anne? This is Mrs Newton." Jamie's mother. Jamie and his sister Lucy are two of my favourite baby-sitting charges.

"Hi!" I said.

"Is everything okay?" asked Mrs Newton.

"Sure," I replied. "Why?"

"Well, it's just that you're never late," she began.

I clapped my hand to my forehead. I'd completely forgotten. I was supposed to sit for Jamie that day. The appointment was written in the record book and everything. How could I have been so stupid?

"I'm sorry!" I cried. "I'll come right over!" And I did.

What a day. It was a good thing I didn't believe in superstition. If I did, I might have blamed the day on the chain letter. And then I would *really* have worried — wondering what sort of bad luck was going to be visited upon my friends and loved ones . . .

(By the way, if you're wondering, I called Logan that night and we made up. Also, the orange juice came out of the dress and didn't leave a stain.)

4th CHAPTER

· Wednesday

Don't laugh, everybody. Looking back on it, I can see that it wasn't a very bright idea.

I baby-sat for Jackie Rodowsky and he and I tried to make his Halloween costume. Dumb idea, huh? You got it.

It was one of those days when I was sitting for just Jackie because his brothers were off taking lessons (piano for Shea, and tumbling for Archie, I think). Anyway, as you know, Jackie alone is about as much trouble as all three boys together. But for some reason, I wasn't remembering that, so when Jackie asked to make his Halloween costume, I agreed to it. And the rest goes down in baby-sitting history....

Jackie didn't even wait until his mother and brothers were in the car before he suggested to poor Dawn that they make his costume. The door to the garage was just closing as he said, "Dawn? I want to be a robot."

Dawn didn't catch on right away. "You want to play robots?" she asked.

"No, I want to *be* a robot. For Halloween. Can we make my costume this afternoon? We've got everything we need."

"Well," said Dawn, who hadn't brought her Kid-Kit and didn't really have anything planned. "I don't see why not."

"Goody!"

"What are you going to make your costume out of?"

"Boxes and jar lids and springs and buttons and googly eyes. Then we'll paint it."

Dawn felt a bit overwhelmed, but she said, "Okay, do you know where everything is?"

"All over the place," he replied.

"Well, let's start rounding it up. And if we're going to paint, we better work in the basement."

"Aw," said Jackie, "it's too cold down there. Let's make the robot here in the sitting room. When he's ready to be painted, then we'll move him to the basement."

"All right," said Dawn.

"Let's get the boxes first," said Jackie, "since they're the most important. They're out in the garage."

Dawn and Jackie went into the garage, and that was where Jackie had his first accident of the day.

I should stop here to tell you a little about Jackie Rodowsky. He and his brothers are some of the club's newest charges. They're look-alikes, with red hair and faces full of freckles. We like them a lot—even Jackie, who is completely accident-prone. Accidents just seem to follow him around and happen to him. I mean, sometimes things occur that he doesn't even have anything to do with. Like he'll be sitting in the living room, and an ashtray will fall off a table in the study. Well, maybe I'm exaggerating. Most of the time, Jackie is a happy-go-lucky bumbler. He gets his hands caught in things, he trips, he falls, he gets locked into places. And sometimes he just plain makes mischief. For instance, there was the time he and his brothers wanted to see what would happen to their socks if the vacuum cleaner sucked them up. (Luckily, not much.)

Jackie is seven, Shea is nine, and little Archie is four. Shea and Archie are not accident-prone, which is why they take lessons and Jackie doesn't. Not that Jackie hasn't tried, but, well, for example, he hadn't been taking piano lessons for very long when he managed to break his teacher's metronome *and* her doorbell. (Don't ask me how.) He may have broken a few other things, too.

Anyway, that's Jackie's story, so now you can see why agreeing to make a robot costume was sort of dangerous. But Dawn had said she'd do it.

Out in the garage, Jackie showed Dawn a huge stack of cardboard boxes. "We can use any of these," he told her.

"Are you sure?" replied Dawn. "What are they here for?"

"Oh, anything. Storing stuff, taking rubbish to the dump, recycling newspapers."

Jackie reached for the biggest box he saw. It was on the bottom of the pile.

THUD, THUD, THUD, KER-RASH!

The mountain of boxes toppled over.

Dawn sighed. Her afternoon was just beginning.

When all but three of the boxes (the big one, a medium-sized one, and a small one) had been stacked again, Dawn and Jackie brought their boxes inside. They set them on the floor.

"Okay," said Dawn. "What else do we need?"

"Paint," replied Jackie.

"I better get that," Dawn said nervously. Jackie showed her where it was, and Dawn put several jars of ready-mixed poster paints, plus some brushes, with the boxes.

"Now," Jackie went on, "we just need *stuff*." He found several jar lids, a coil of wire, and an old Slinky toy on shelves in the basement. In a box marked SCRAPS he found some pieces of felt, five wooden cotton reels, and the googly eyes he'd been talking about.

"See?" he said, holding up the plastic eyes with the moving black pupils. "We got a whole package of these once. They're googly."

Dawn had to agree.

"Last thing," Jackie continued. "Buttons. They're upstairs in Mum's sewing chest."

Dawn made the mistake of letting Jackie go upstairs alone. How much trouble, she thought, could he get into with buttons? They weren't messy or dangerous or—

KER-RASH.

Dawn closed her eyes for a moment to collect her thoughts before she headed upstairs. When she reached Mr and Mrs Rodowsky's bedroom, she found Jackie kneeling by the overturned sewing chest. Needles and pins and reels of thread and packets of zips and piles of buttons were scattered across the rug.

"Oops," said Jackie.

It took more than fifteen minutes for Dawn and Jackie to put each item back into its little compartment. Then Dawn insisted on vacuuming the rug, in case they'd missed a stray pin or needle. Jackie wanted to start on his robot while Dawn vacuumed, but by then, she knew better.

"You sit right there," she told him, pointing to his parents' bed, "until I've

finished. Then we'll go downstairs together."

At long last, they began work on the
robot. Dawn had sensibly spread newspapers over the floor before Jackie opened
the bottle of Elmer's glue.

"See, what we do," Jackie said, "is glue
these two boxes together to make the body.
Then we put dials and stuff all over it—
those are the jar lids and buttons and things.
And then we make a robot head—well, a hat
really—out of the little box. I want to put
the Slinky on top of the hat."

"We better paint the boxes before you
glue things on them," Dawn pointed out.

"Oh, right," said Jackie. "But first, I
have to make the body." He got busy with
the boxes and glue. He cut a neckhole. He
cut two armholes. Then he cut himself.

"Ow!"

Dawn fixed up his bleeding thumb with
antiseptic cream and a plaster.

Then Jackie glued the boxes together.
"Now for the paint," he announced.

Dawn helped him carry the boxes to the
basement — ever so carefully, since the glue
wasn't dry. After Jackie had knocked over a
jar of blue paint and he and Dawn had
mopped it up, he painted his robot a wild
array of colours. The poster paints dried
quickly.

They carried the robot back upstairs.

"Okay, this is the fun part," said Jackie.

And he proceeded to turn the painted cartons into a really splendid robot.

Even though every other word out of his mouth was, "Whoops," he managed to glue the jar lids and reels and buttons all over the body of the robot. Using a fat felt-tip, he drew a gauge and a needle (measuring . . . what?) on the robot's belly. He attached wires, coiled to look like springs. To the head, he glued two googly eyes and the Slinky. He couldn't find a use for the felt scraps, but it was almost time for Mrs Rodowsky and Shea and Archie to come home, anyway.

"Hey!" he cried. "I know! I'll put my costume on so I can surprise them when they walk through the door."

Dawn smiled. "Good idea." She was relieved that the rest of the project had gone so peacefully and safely.

Jackie slipped the boxes over his head. His put on his hat and grinned at Dawn. He was the perfect homemade robot.

For three seconds.

Then his hat fell off. The top of the body came apart from the bottom part of the body, and the bottom dropped to the floor, like the stages of a rocket separating. The reels and jar lids and wires and googly eyes came off and rolled under the couch.

"Oh, no!" cried Dawn.

But Jackie just said calmly, "Oops. I guess the glue wasn't dry. Poor old robot.

35

I'll put him back together tomorrow."

What bad luck, Dawn thought, as she rode her bike home that afternoon. Briefly, she remembered my chain letter and wondered if maybe I shouldn't have broken the chain. Maybe bad luck was being visited upon her, since she's one of my friends. Then, no, she realized. Jackie always has bad luck. He's a walking disaster.

Dawn forgot about the chain letter.

5th
CHAPTER

Another Friday, another club meeting. After baby-sitting for two little girls, Nina and Eleanor Marshall (I remembered my appointment that day), I checked our mailbox before going to the Kishis'. And in among the bills and magazines I found a small package!

I closed my hands over it, hoping it was for me. But it was probably for Dad. My birthday was over, Christmas was two months away, and I hadn't ordered anything from the back of a magazine lately. Maybe it was a free sample. That could be interesting, especially if it was hand lotion or make-up or shampoo.

I opened my hands. The package *was* for me! And it wasn't just a sample. But right away, I felt those chills again. My name and address were made out of letters cut from magazines and newspapers. It was the kind of thing you only see on TV or in the movies when somebody has been kidnapped and the bad guys mail a ransom note. I know it sounds crazy, but my first thought was that Tigger had been kittennapped. I ran inside to check him.

"Tigger! Tigger!" I called.

I found him curled up in a ball of rumbly purrs on the living room sofa.

"Oh, thank goodness!" I exclaimed, letting out a lungful of air. "You're here and you're alive."

I raced over to Claudia's, the box clutched in my hand.

Kristy and Claudia were the only club members there, and Kristy was the one who noticed immediately that the box was addressed not just to me but to:

There was no return address.

The three of us looked at each other. I could see fear in my friends' eyes, and I'm sure they could see it in mine. We were dying to open the box (and at the same time afraid to), but we waited until Dawn, Jessi, and Mal arrived before we did.

Kristy was so nervous about what might be inside that she didn't even conduct an official meeting. In fact, she forgot to put on her visor, and she crowded onto the bed with Dawn and Claudia and me.

"We'll just take phone calls today," she informed us. "We can take care of business on Monday."

We all looked at the box.

"Well," I said, "who's going to open it?"

"You, of course," said Kristy. "It was in your mailbox, and it's addressed mostly to you."

"You're afraid!" I cried. I was relieved to find I had company.

"You're right."

I scowled. "Okay." I began to peel back the paper as slowly and as carefully as if a bomb might be inside. (And these days, who knew?)

I unwound one layer of paper, then another, then a third. Inside lay a harmless white jewellery box.

I gave my friends a look that said, "We are all such idiots. We've been afraid of jewellery."

But Jessi didn't look a bit relieved. "Anything could be inside," she pointed out. "And there are a lot of anythings I wouldn't want to be within a mile of."

My fear returned.

With shaking hands I lifted the lid of the box.

All I could see was tissue paper.

"Claudia? Do you have any tweezers?" I asked. "I'm not touching this."

"Oh, for heaven's sake." Claudia took the box from me and pulled the tissue paper up. She crumpled it into a ball, which she dropped on the bed.

"Ew!" shrieked Dawn, jumping away from the paper, and the rest of us screamed, too.

When we calmed down, we dared—all six of us—to peer into the box.

"What is it?" asked Mallory.

"It looks like a necklace," I replied.

Lying in the box was a tiny glass ball on a delicate gold chain. The ball was hollow, and inside was what looked like a seed—a small, blah, yellowish-brown thing.

I lifted the necklace out, afraid that at any moment it might go up in a puff of smoke, or that *we* might go up in a puff of smoke.

"It's kind of pretty." Claudia interrupted my thoughts. "Really. It's weird-looking and it's unusual. I like it because it's different. It's my kind of jewellery."

I was about to tell her she could have it,

when I realized what it had been resting on in the box. It wasn't your usual little piece of cotton.

"Hey, here's a note!" I exclaimed.

"Oh, brother. Which one of us is going to read it?" asked Dawn.

"I—I guess I better," I said. "I mean, Kristy's right. The box was mostly addressed to me."

I dropped the necklace on the bed (everyone scrambled away from it), and opened up the note.

"Handwriting?" asked Kristy.

I shook my head. "Nope. More cut-out letters from the newspaper."

"So what does it say?" asked Claudia.

"It—it says," I replied shakily, "well, see for yourselves."

I spread open the note on Claudia's bed. The members of the Babysitters Club leaned over to look at it, although I noticed that nobody got too close. The note said:

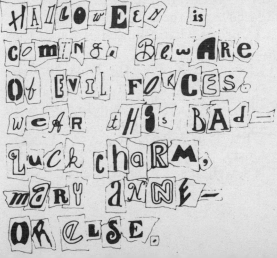

HALLOWEEN is coming. BewARe Of EVIL FOrCES. WEAR tHIs BAD— LuCK chaRM, mARY aNNE— OR ELSE.

"Augh!" I shrieked.

"Bad-luck charm?" cried Mallory with a gasp. "Oh, I knew it. I just knew it."

I looked at the necklace, which was lying on the bed near the note. "Oh, my gosh, I've already touched it," I said.

"Touched it," Dawn repeated. "You've got to *wear* it."

"Are you crazy? No way!" I exclaimed.

"I think you better," said Jessi. "Are you going to ignore this warning . . . like you ignored the chain letter?"

I looked at the older girls. After all, Mal and Jessi are two years younger than the rest of us. Of course they believed in warnings and charms.

But my friends were no help.

"May-maybe you ought to wear it," said Dawn.

"Yeah . . ." said Claudia slowly.

"I thought you guys didn't believe in superstitious stuff!" I cried. The thing was, I sort of believed it myself. Otherwise I would have put the necklace on right away, just to prove what a bunch of dopes they were.

I glanced at Kristy. She looked embarrassed. I realized that for once she wasn't scoffing. She wasn't laughing, either. In fact, she looked pretty scared.

"What is it with you guys?" I asked nervously.

"It's, well, it's . . ." Dawn began. "See, I

42

had some pretty bad luck with Jackie Rodowsky yesterday." She told us about his unfortunate robot and all the accidents.

"But Jackie is bad luck, just like you said," I told her.

"This was worse than usual," Dawn replied. "It was a pretty bad baby-sitting experience."

"I failed a spelling test," added Claudia.

"You always fail spelling tests," I said.

"Not lately." Claudia looked haughty.

"I fell in ballet class," said Jessi. "That never happens."

"I lost my watch," said Kristy.

"I got in trouble for talking during maths," said Mal.

"You know what?" Claud added. "Stacey called a while ago. She broke her dad's paper-weight. That one he loves. She can't even figure out how to confess to him."

"Well, I might as well tell you," I went on. "I had the worst day of my life the day after I threw away the chain letter." I described the day, from falling out of bed to forgetting my baby-sitting job. When I was done, we all just stared at each other. At long last, I picked up the charm and slipped it over my head.

"This thing scares me to death," I admitted. "It's *bad luck*. But what would happen if I *didn't* wear it? Things might be worse than bad."

"Evil," said Mal in a whisper.

43

"But who sent the charm?" I wondered. None of us had any ideas.

"And why did they send it to me? Why do *I* have to wear the thing?"

"Maybe," answered Jessi, "because you were the one who threw the chain letter away. This is your bad luck. And all the other stuff is the bad luck that's being visited upon your friends."

"What about the rest of the note?" I asked.

" 'Halloween is coming. Beware of evil forces.' What's that supposed to mean?"

"Well," said Claudia, "Halloween is the spookiest, eeriest time of year."

"But the evil forces—" I began.

"I think," said Mal, "that we will have to ward them off."

We all knew that wouldn't be easy. I had broken a good-luck chain and was wearing a bad-luck charm. I couldn't change either situation.

Still, we did have to ward off the evil forces. The question was—how?

6th
CHAPTER

I was terrified.

Who wouldn't be?

On Saturday, the day after I got the bad-luck charm, I was wearing it while I sat for Jamie Newton. Jamie spilled everything in sight, dropped everything in sight, and then fell and skinned his knee. And he didn't just trip and fall. He fell down half a flight of steps. Of course, he cried. A lot. But a plaster helped. Jamie likes plasters!

On Monday, the first day I wore the charm to school, there was a fire in a rubbish bin (which the fire brigade had to come and put out), an explosion in the science lab (no one was hurt, but a bunsen burner was completely destroyed), and an accident in a gym class. (Miranda Shillaber twisted her ankle. She had to go to the nurse and she needed a bandage and everything.)

"Maybe," said Kristy at lunch that day,

45

"this is just a big coincidence."

I looked around at Kristy, Claudia, Dawn and Logan. They were all picking at their food. So was I. The hot vegetable that day was mixed beans, and therefore looked incredibly disgusting, but Kristy hadn't made a single comment about it. So I knew she didn't believe what she'd just said. She was too worried and preoccupied even to try to make me sick.

I glanced down at the charm. The little seed was resting on the bottom of its glass globe. I decided that it looked like something that was carefully, calmly planning horrible deeds.

"One accident on the first day I wear the charm," I said, "might be a coincidence. One little spill at the Newtons'. But not spills and broken stuff and Jamie's knee. I could even accept one little fire at school that Mr Halprin puts out by himself with a bucket of water. That could still be a coincidence. But not a fire-brigade fire—"

"And an explosion," continued Logan.

"*Plus* a gym injury," finished Dawn.

"Right," I agreed. And then I went on in a whisper, "You know what else? There have been other signs of bad luck today."

"There *have*?" Kristy replied. "Like what?"

"My father opened an umbrella in the house this morning."

Kristy rolled her eyes.

"But wait, there's more," I said. "On the way to school, a black cat crossed our path."* I glanced at Claudia, who nodded nervously.

"That's right, one did," she said.

"And just before I came into the dining room?" I went on.

"Yeah?" said Logan. He reached over and held onto my hand. I wasn't sure if he wanted to comfort me, or if he was afraid himself.

"I saw a penny on the floor, so I bent down and picked it up. I just did it without thinking. It was already in my hand before I realized it was a *tail-up* penny. I dropped it, but by then it was too late."

Our table was silent. On another day, any one of those bad-luck signs would have made us laugh. But today—the first day I wore the charm to school—three signs, three accidents, the charm, and the chain letter were just too much.

"You know what?" I said after a moment. "This charm is a curse. And we have to do something about it."

"That's what Mallory said on Friday," Kristy pointed out. "Remember? She said we had to ward off the evil forces."

"How?" Claudia demanded to know.

Not one of us had an answer. Especially not Logan, who was looking at us as if we

*This is bad luck in America.

were all crazy. Who could blame him? I was willing to bet that over at Grace and Cokie's table, they weren't talking about charms and curses and evil forces. They were probably talking about the Halloween Hop.

I glanced at them. Five people were at Grace's table—Grace, Cokie, and three of the girls in their group of friends. They were staring at our table. I felt my face grow hot.

"Shh, you guys," I hissed. "I think we're talking too loudly. People are listening."

"It's no wonder," whispered Dawn. "This is probably the most fascinating conversation they've heard in weeks."

Kristy, Claudia, Dawn, and I began to giggle. Cokie and her friends couldn't stop staring at us, though, and Logan began to get that I've-had-enough-of-girls look. He escaped to a tableful of boys.

"Let's continue this discussion," said Dawn, "but keep our voices down."

"All right," the rest of us agreed.

"We've got a little problem," Dawn went on. "Okay. Mary Anne has a charm. The note that came with it said it's a bad-luck charm."

"Right."

"And we didn't really know whether to believe that until today," Kristy added. "Now, Mary Anne has worn the charm to the Newtons' and had bad luck there and worn the charm to school and found bad luck at school."

48

"There seems to be bad luck wherever I wear the charm. In fact, there's bad luck wherever *I* am," I said.

My friends all edged away from me, sliding their lunches down the table.

"Thanks a lot!" I exclaimed.

The others looked embarrassed, but they didn't apologize or move back.

"Does anybody know anything about charms and curses?" asked Claudia.

We all shook our heads.

"I read a Nancy Drew book once called *The Mystery of the Ivory Charm,*" Claudia, our mystery-lover, went on, "but I don't think it would help us." She paused thoughtfully. "Well," she said at last, "how can we find out about charms and curses and evil forces? We've got to do something."

"We better go to the library," I replied.

"Oh, I *hate* the library!" cried Claudia.

"Even when you're not there for a school assignment?" I asked her. "Even when you're just there on your own?"

Claudia made a face.

"Well, I think we should go anyway," I pronounced. "And I think we should ask Jessi and Mal to come with us. Claudia can go or not go. It's up to her."

"No, it isn't," spoke up Kristy. "It's not up to her. She's going."

"I am?" said Claudia. "How come?"

"Because this club sticks together," was

Kristy's reply. "We'll meet at the front doors to the school as soon as the last bell has rung."

End of discussion.

And that was exactly what we did. Even Jessi, who has her steady sitting job on Mondays and Wednesdays, was able to go to the library, since the Braddock kids were sick with the flu. I invited Logan to join us, but he said he wouldn't be able to go. I guess the thought of being with six girls who were doing research on witchcraft was too much for him.

Even though I was wearing the bad-luck charm and it was really frightening me, I daydreamed contentedly all the way to the library. I kept thinking about books I'd read in which kids go to the library on just this sort of mission, and when they ask the librarian (who is always a white-haired woman about ninety years old) for books on witchcraft, she takes them to some musty old corner of the library (maybe even to the basement) and shows them these big, scary, dusty books that are older than she is. The books are weird, a little *too* helpful, and no one seems to know where they came from.

Well, our visit to the Stoneybrook Public Library wasn't like that at all.

"What do we do first?" Claudia whispered, as soon as we were inside.

I looked around for a white-haired,

ninety-year-old woman. "Ask the librarian," I replied.

"No, we don't have to do that," said Mal and Jessi at the same time. (Since they both like to read, they probably go to the library a lot.)

"We can just go to the card catalogue," Jessi added.

"Children's room or adults'?" asked Kristy.

"Adults'," our experts replied immediately. "We'll find much better stuff in the adult section."

"More informative," Mal added importantly. "But we really have to behave and act grown-up. Librarians are always suspicious of kids in the adult section."

Mal and Jessi led the way to the adult card catalogue. Under the heading "Witchcraft", we found cards for tons of books.

"Do we have to copy down *all* of these numbers and look up *each* of these books?" asked Claudia. "I think I'm getting a headache. I better go home."

"*No way*," said Kristy flatly.

"Besides," I added, "we don't have to look for each book separately. They're in the same section. See? The numbers all start out the same way. If we find this area, we'll have found the right section. That's all we need."

Mal and Jessi looked at me admiringly. Their admiration was nice, but I felt like saying, "I know how to use the library, too, you know."

Considering that the Stoneybrook Public Library is a modern building that was put up just eight years ago, after the town outgrew the old library, I don't know why I thought the witchcraft books would be in a lost, dusty, spooky corner. The new library doesn't have any lost, dusty, spooky corners. The witchcraft books are just in a row of other books on metal shelves under a buzzing fluorescent light.

One piece of good luck was that they were on the bottom shelf, so we could sit on the floor. We began pulling the books out and looking through their tables of contents.

"Here's one called *On Witchcraft*," I said.

"Here's one called *Witches Through the Ages*," Dawn said a moment later.

"Here's one called *Strange Phenomena*," Jessi spoke up.

"And here's one called *Charms and Spells*," said Kristy.

"Why do we need all this witch and spell stuff?" I wondered out loud.

"How else are we going to ward off the evil forces of the charm?" asked Mal.

I shook my head. "I don't know. I thought none of us knew. That's why we're here."

"Well, it has to be some sort of spell, doesn't it?" Mal replied. "I figured we just didn't know which one."

I shivered. "Okay. A spell."

We turned back to the books. I began to imagine midnight and a full moon, the six of us mixing up herbs and weird, hard-to-find things, and chanting a spooky rhyme.

"Maybe we ought to ask Karen for advice," I said, smiling.

"*Oh, no!*" cried Kristy. Her little step-sister is totally into ghosts and witches. She even thinks that Mrs Porter, the old woman who lives next door to Kristy, is actually a witch named Morbidda Destiny. "She'd never leave us alone if she knew what we were up to."

I wished I knew what we were up to. But I didn't. Not really. So I turned back to the books. At five o'clock we each chose one to check out. Then we made a dash for Claudia's house and our club meeting.

7th CHAPTER

Thursday

Halloween is supposed to be scary, but I never realized just how scary it can be for some little kids. I was sitting for Jamie Newton today, and it turns out that he's totally freaked-out by Halloween. Everything scares him. Don't ask me why, but he's afraid of trick-or-treaters. He's even afraid of the costume parade that's going to be held at his nursery school. (Or at least he was when I first got to his house. He didn't have a costume, either, because he said he was afraid to dress up.)

Jessi was right. Jamie was spooked. (So were all us baby-sitters—but for a different reason.)

As Mrs Newton was leaving that afternoon, she said to Jessi in a low voice, "I hope everything will be okay. This is the first year Halloween has meant much to Jamie" (Jamie is four) "and he's terrified. Mr Newton and I have tried to make it sound like fun, but Jamie has only picked up on the scary stuff."

Jessi nodded. "Okay. Thanks for telling me."

(We sitters appreciate parents who warn us about problems that might come up while we're in charge.)

Then Mrs Newton left with Lucy, Jamie's baby sister, who was getting over an ear infection and had an appointment with the doctor.

"Well, Jamie," said Jessi, as Mrs Newton's car was backing into the street, "what do you want to do today?"

Sometimes it's not a good idea to ask an open-ended question like that. I mean, what if the kid's reply is that he wants to skate around the kitchen floor on bars of soap—or do something even worse? But when you're familiar with the kid you're sitting for, you also know when it's okay to ask such a question. And Jessi had sat for Jamie a few times and knew that he wouldn't suggest anything weird.

"I want to . . . I want to . . . I don't know . . ." said Jamie vaguely.

Jessi began to wish that she'd brought her Kid-Kit along. A sort of unspoken rule among us baby-sitters is that you always spend time with the kids you're sitting for, unless you're being paid extra to be a parents' helper and are supposed to be washing dishes or folding clothes or something. This might seem sort of obvious, but you'd be surprised at how many sitters just wait until the parents leave and then park themselves in front of the TV until they return, never paying a bit of attention to the kids.

Jessi had no intention of doing that. (None of us would.) "You want to play outside?" she asked Jamie.

Jamie shook his head, his eyes growing big and frightened.

"What's wrong?" asked Jessi.

"Trick-or-treaters might come by."

"Oh, not today, Jamie," Jessi assured him. "It isn't Halloween yet. There won't be any trick-or-treaters until Halloween."

"I hope it's never Halloween," said Jamie.

Jessi led Jamie to the sofa in the living room and sat him down.

"What are you so afraid of?" she asked.

"Halloween," Jamie replied simply.

"But Halloween is fun," said Jessi. "Honest. Everyone gets sweets, and you dress up. You could be a ghost, or a witch—"

Jamie covered his eyes with his hands. "No!"

"Or Superman," Jessi went on.

"No ghosts! No witches!" Jamie cried.

"But they aren't real," Jessi told him. "They're just people dressed up."

"Ghosts and witches scare me. Especially ghosts."

"Why?"

"They just scare me."

"Not all ghosts are mean," said Jessi. And that was when she had her brainstorm. "Hey," she said excitedly, "did you ever hear of Georgie?"

"Georgie?" Jamie repeated.

"Yeah," said Jessi. "He was a ghost—a little ghost—and he was very shy. As shy as a mouse. He didn't like loud noises or too much confusion. He lived in the attic of Mr and Mrs Whittaker's house, and all he wanted was peace and quiet. And to be with his friends, Herman and Miss Oliver."

"Who are the Whittakers?" Jamie asked. "And who are Herman and Miss Oliver?"

"If you really want to know," said Jessi, "we could go over to my house and I could show you some of the books about Georgie."

"Well..." said Jamie, who looked pretty interested in spite of himself, "okay."

So Jessi buttoned Jamie into his jacket (a button came off in her hand), and retied his trainers (one of the laces broke as she did so), and nearly had a heart attack.

It's the bad luck! she thought wildly. It's Mary Anne's bad luck being visited upon her friends again. In the moments that followed, Jessi panicked—but only in her mind. The Braddock kids have the flu, she thought, and Lucy Newton has had an earache—that's a lot of sickness—and Jamie is overreacting to Halloween. And now the button and the shoelace. (Not to mention everything else that had happened.)

Jessi took two deep breaths and tried to calm down.

Jamie was looking at her oddly.

"Okay," said Jessi briskly. "If you'll show me where the sewing box is, and if you know where the extra shoelaces are, I'll fix you up and then we'll go over to my house and find the Georgie books."

Which is exactly what they did.

When Jamie was ready, Jessi left a note for Mrs Newton, saying where they were going (in case Mrs Newton came home early), and then she and Jamie left the house. Jessi carefully locked the door behind her.

On the way to the Ramseys', Jamie asked, "Is there anybody my age where you live?"

Jessi shook her head. "Sorry, Jamie. My sister Becca is eight, and then I have a baby brother, Squirt."

"A baby?" said Jamie. "Like Lucy?"

"Yes, but a little older. Squirt's almost walking."

58

Jamie nodded. "Whose are the Georgie books?"

"Well," replied Jessi, "they used to be mine, and now they're Becca's, but they're waiting to be Squirt's. They're perfect for someone who's four years old, though. Just like you. That's why I think you'll like them."

"Hello?" called a voice when Jessi opened the front door to her house.

"Hi, Mama. It's me," Jessi replied. "I brought Jamie Newton over for a few minutes. We're going to look at some books."

Mrs Ramsey appeared in the front hall. "Hi, Jamie," she said.

"Hi," Jamie answered shyly.

"I'll explain later," Jessi whispered to her mother as she and Jamie scooted by her on their way to the stairs. Then, "Be careful," she warned Jamie as he started up the staircase. These days, she thought, you really can't be too careful.

"Where are the books?" Jamie asked when he was safely upstairs.

"In Becca's room," Jessi replied.

The door to Becca's room was open, so Jessi went in, scanned her sister's bookcase, and found a skinny picture book. She handed it to Jamie, and the two of them went into Jessi's room to read.

"This book," said Jessi, "is called *Georgie's Halloween*."

"Uh-oh," moaned Jamie.

"No, it's okay. Really," Jessi told him. "We'll just look at the pictures first. Here. See these old people?"

"Are they Mr and Mrs Whittaker?" asked Jamie.

"That's right," Jessi replied. "And here are Herman and Miss Oliver."

"Herman's a cat and Miss Oliver's an owl!" Jamie exclaimed.

"Yup. And here's Georgie."

"*That* little thing?" said Jamie, pointing to one of the pictures. "But he doesn't look mean at all. He's smiling."

"He isn't mean," said Jessi. "Remember? He's even shy." And then Jessi read Jamie the story about the little ghost who was *so* shy that he wouldn't enter the town's contest for best Halloween costume, even though he would have won, hands down.

"Well, that's silly," said Jamie when the story was over. "*I* would have entered the contest."

"You can be in your costume parade at school," Jessi pointed out.

Jamie looked thoughtful. "Maybe," he said at last. "I wonder . . ."

"You wonder what?"

"If Mummy could make me a Georgie costume."

"You want to be a ghost?"

"No. Georgie. Only Georgie. Then if there are any prizes, maybe I'll win. I mean,

60

Georgie could win. He could win his prize after all."

"Now that," said Jessi, "is a great idea." She and Jamie smiled at each other.

"Any more Georgie books?" asked Jamie.

"Yup."

"Well . . . let's read them!"

8th CHAPTER

Oh my lord that was my werst siting experience ever.

Claudia, it wasn't that bad.

Yes it was mal. Just count up all the things that whent wronge.

Okay. Well, there was the dinner.

And the bird

Right, the bird. And Vanessa's tooth.

I think the tooth was the werst. Because of the bloode.

The blood was bad, but the bird thing took so long to solve. And it made the triplets crazy.

Well lets not arg How on erth do you spell Arque?

Right.

62

It was another one of those long two-person entries. They turn up in the notebook every now and then—when we're taking care of the Pike brood (they usually need two sitters), or if Jessi and Mal are sitting together, which happens sometimes, since they're younger.

This entry was from a Saturday—two days after Jessi convinced Jamie that not all ghosts are scary. Claudia and Mallory sat for Mallory's brothers and sisters.

It was quite an ordeal. Really, as much as I like Mallory and her levelheadedness, I have to take Claudia's side here. It *was* her worst baby-sitting experience ever. I'm even willing to go out on a limb and say that it was the worst experience any of us has ever had. Maybe it wasn't as frightening as the time Dawn thought Buddy Barrett had been kidnapped, or the time I had to get Jenny Prezzioso to the hospital in an ambulance, but, well, so *many* things went wrong. And so many things went so *very* wrong.

I might as well get it all out in the open here. Us sitters agreed that this was more bad luck being visited upon my friends. The spate of bad luck was hard to ignore. It wasn't just a little accident here, a piece of unwelcome news there; it was one bad thing after another. Even bad things with Stacey in New York.

Mr and Mrs Pike hadn't been gone for

five minutes when the first bad thing happened. The Pikes were out for a long, late evening, so Claudia and Mal had a big night ahead of them, starting with giving the Pike kids their dinner. Mr Pike had cooked up a batch of some sort of casserole with sausage pieces in it. Claudia thought it looked revolting, so she, personally, wasn't too upset about what happened a few minutes later, but the Pikes—even Mallory —*were*. Apparently this dish is special to them. They call it Daddy Stew. And they were really looking forward to it, especially Byron, who loves to eat. He's sort of a human vacuum cleaner.

Before I get any further, I suppose I should remind you about Mallory's brothers and sisters, since the Pikes are not your average family.

Mallory is the oldest, of course, and she's eleven. The triplets she wrote about in the notebook are her ten-year-old brothers,— Byron, Jordan, and Adam. They're identical, and they can be a handful. They like to tease, especially their younger brother Nicky, but they're basically good kids. Vanessa is nine. She's a budding poet and sometimes talks in rhyme, which could drive you crazy. Nicky is eight. He's also a good kid but has trouble fitting in with his family. His brothers think he's a baby, and Nicky hates girls, which is a problem. Margo Pike is seven and going through a bossy stage. Last but not least is Claire, who's five and sometimes really plays up her baby-of-the-family role. What a family.

Okay, back to the Daddy Stew. Mr and Mrs Pike had just left. The last thing Mrs Pike said before the door closed behind her was, "Let the Daddy Stew heat up until six-thirty. Leave the burner where it is."

"Six-thirty!" Byron exclaimed. "I can't wait that long!"

"That's less than half an hour from now," Mallory pointed out.

"But I'm *starving*. I'll die of starvation before then!"

"No, you won't. Come on. Help us get ready in the play room. We're not going to eat in the kitchen tonight. We're going to have an indoor picnic."

"An indoor picnic!" cried the other Pikes. "Goody!" They got busy carrying things down to the play room, then spreading a tablecloth on the floor and laying out the plates and forks and spoons and napkins.

Byron never joined them. No one paid any attention to that. Not until they noticed an awful acrid smell — like smoking rubber.

Claudia sniffed the air. "Is something burning?" she asked worriedly.

Mallory sniffed, too. "Uh-oh," she said.

Claudia, Mallory, Adam, Jordan, Vanessa, Nicky, Margo, and Claire raced upstairs to the kitchen. On the stove was a smoking pot of Daddy Stew. Byron was standing next to it. He looked from the pot to his baby-sitters.

"Oops," he said.

Mallory dashed to the stove and turned the burner off. Then she grabbed a pot-holder and lifted the lid. The Daddy Stew was a horrid, burned, black mess.

"Ew! Ew! Pee-yew!" cried the Pike kids. They held their noses and backed out of the kitchen.

"The Daddy Stew is *ruined*, Mallory. Byron *ruined* it," cried Claire.

"I'm sorry," said Byron. "Honest. I was hungry. And I just thought that if I turned the fire up—"

"Aughh! Aughh!"

Shrieks were coming from the living room, where the Pikes (except for Mal and Byron) had fled to escape the smell of the ruined Daddy Stew.

"Now what?" exclaimed Claudia.

"I don't know," Mallory replied, shaking her head, "but that sounded like more than just a stop-teasing-me-or-I'll-kill-you scream. I think something happened."

The girls left the kitchen (Claudia calling over her shoulder, "You're in charge of cleaning up that mess, Byron!") and hurried into the living room. They found the Pikes running back and forth, stooped over, as if the ceiling were closing in on them.

Above them flew a bird.

"Oh, my lord!" cried Claudia. "Where did that come from?"

"It flew down the chimney!" Vanessa shrieked. "Aughh! Oh, help!"

"Now, wait a sec, guys. That bird is scared to death and you're scaring it even more," said Mallory sensibly. "So either calm down and help Claudia and me, or go and watch TV."

Vanessa made a dash for the TV. Everyone else stayed. They huddled around Claud and Mal in the entryway to the living room.

The poor bird, which was only a little sparrow, kept letting out terrified sparrow-squawks and swooping from one side of the living room to the other.

"How are we going to catch him?" asked Nicky.

"Maybe it's a 'her'," said Adam, just to torture Nicky.

"Never mind that," Mallory told Adam. "We have to keep the bird from flying into something, like the window. It could knock itself out."

"Hey!" said Jordan. "Maybe if we open the windows and doors, the bird will just fly outside."

"I could get my butterfly net," said Nicky. "Maybe I could scoop it up. Then we could take it outdoors and let it loose."

"Yeah, right," said Jordan sarcastically.

"Maybe it'll calm down and land somewhere," suggested Margo. "We could throw a pillowcase over it."

"I wonder if the bird knows Santa Claus," Claire said dreamily.

Everyone forgot about the sparrow for a moment.

"Huh?" said Adam.

"The bird came down the chimney, just like Santa," Claire explained. "I wonder . . ."

Adam, Jordan, and Nicky snickered behind their hands.

Then, "Aughh!" Margo shrieked again as the bird made another arc across the living room, just inches above her head.

"Okay, we're wasting time," said Mallory. "Let's open the windows and doors. That seems like the best idea so far."

Claudia and the Pikes rushed around, opening every window and door on that level of the house.

"Go ahead, little birdie," Margo coaxed the sparrow. Then suddenly, feeling brave (or maybe bossy), she raised her hands in the air and ran toward a window, waving and screaming. "Get out of here, bird!"

The sparrow flew ahead of her—and went right out the window.

"Good job!" Mallory exclaimed. "Thanks, Margo."

"Whew," said Claudia. "All right. Let's close everything up."

Claudia turned around to go back to the

kitchen and was met by the sight of Vanessa holding blood-smeared hands to her mouth.

"Oh, my lord!" cried Claudia, who was getting a lot of mileage out of that phrase that evening. "Vanessa, what happened?"

As Vanessa let Claudia guide her toward the sink in the kitchen, she held out her hand. In it was a small, bloody tooth.

"I didn't know you had a loose tooth, Vanessa," said Mallory.

"I didn't know I did, either," Vanessa replied tearfully. Claudia helped her to rinse out her mouth with warm, salty water. When the bleeding had stopped, Vanessa said sheepishly, "I was eating a piece of candy. It was really sticky. I bit down on it, and when I opened my mouth again, the candy pulled the tooth out."

Well, as you can imagine, it was a while before Claudia and the Pikes sat down to their indoor picnic. The kids, especially the triplets, were wild over the bird and Vanessa's mouth. Furthermore, it took a while to make eighteen tunafish sandwiches (two apiece), which was the only thing everyone would agree to eat, given the disappointment over the Daddy Stew.

The rest of the evening was uneventful— until Mr and Mrs Pike were an hour late getting home. Claudia was exhausted, and Mallory was nearly hysterical, wondering why her parents hadn't called. It turned out that they'd been caught in a traffic jam on the motorway and *couldn't* call.

If any of us club members had any doubts left about the power of the chain letter, the doubts were gone after Claudia and Mal's sitting experience. We were in big trouble, all of us. And it was my fault.

I had brought bad luck to myself, my friends, and everyone I knew.

9th CHAPTER

"This," said Kristy sombrely, "is an emergency meeting of the Babysitters Club. You all know why you've been called here."

It was Sunday afternoon. The six main members of the club were in Claudia's room in our usual places. And, yes, we all knew why we had been called there.

Because of me. Because I had tempted fate, thrown away a chain letter, and then been sent a bad-luck charm, which I was forced to wear or else. Not knowing what that "or else" meant was the only thing that kept me wearing the charm. Or else death? Death and destruction? Death, destruction, and the end of civilization as we know it? Claudia was afraid it could mean the end of junk food. Who knew? We weren't taking chances. We'd done enough of that already.

"So," said Kristy, "something must be done about Mary Anne's, um, problem."

(If you'll remember, the chain letter had been met by a lot of scepticism at first. Kristy had been the biggest sceptic of all. She'd had no use for charms or spells or bad-luck wishes. She'd scoffed at it all. Now she was as big a believer in such things as Jessi and Mal were. So were the rest of us.)

"Well," said Mallory, "we've got the books. We'd better start going through them. I think a spell to—to, oh, what's the word?"

"Get rid of the bad stuff?" suggested Claudia.

"No, to counteract—that's it, counteract —the bad-luck charm is our only hope."

"Okay, then let's hit the books," said Kristy. The books had all been left in Claudia's room, much to her dismay. We each took the one we'd checked out of the library and began thumbing through it.

"Hey, Claud," I said, "have you noticed these books doing anything weird? Like flying around the room at night, or glowing in the dark?"

Claudia started to laugh, but Kristy glared at both of us. "You cannot," she told us, "afford to take this lightly. Mary Anne, you got us into this mess, so you sure better help us get out of it."

I felt the way I did when I'd forgotten my maths homework and the teacher scolded me in front of the whole class.

"Sorry," I said.

"Sorry," Claudia said.

Embarrassed silence followed. The five of us went back to our books. Occasionally, somebody would turn a page. There was no other sound in the room.

"This is making me crazy!" Claudia cried after a few minutes. She jumped off the bed, opened one of the desk drawers, and pulled out a packet of Rolos. She made a lot of racket rummaging around in the drawer and even more noise crinkling paper as she opened the bag.

"Rolo anyone?" said our junk-food lover.

Claudia has stuff—candy, crisps, gum, you name it—hidden throughout her room. Her parents don't like her to eat junk food, but Claudia doesn't know what she'd do without it. So she hides it. She's got stuff in drawers, behind cushions, under her mattress, in shoe boxes. She's crazy. But we love her anyway.

We each took a Rolo, except for Dawn, who said it would rot her teeth.

"The rest of you will be wearing dentures when you're ninety," she told us. "But I'll still have all my own teeth."

"If I live to be ninety," said Claudia, "I'll just be glad to be alive, teeth or no teeth. You know—"

Claudia broke off when she realized that Kristy was glaring again.

"Okay, okay, okay," said Claudia.

We stuffed the Rolos in our mouths and got back to work.

"Well," said Jessi after a long time, "here's a spell for turning bad luck to good luck. Maybe that would work."

"Sure!" we cried. We all leaned over to look at Jessi's book. Except for Kristy, who was in the director's chair.

"What does it say?" Kristy asked. "I can't see it from over here. Read it aloud."

"Okay," replied Jessi. " 'To reverse the course of luck, press a white rose between the pages of a book of sorcery. After waiting two months—'"

"White rose!" cried Kristy. "Book of sorcery! Two months! This is not rose season, we don't have a book of sorcery—not a real one—and we can't wait two months."

"Well, ex*cuse me*," said Jessi. "I can't help what the book says.

"Hey!" I exclaimed a moment later. "Here's a love spell!"

"A love spell?" repeated Dawn.

"Yeah, you know, to get a guy you like to fall for you. All you need is a lock of his hair, a fingernail clipping, one of his eyelashes—"

"MARY ANNE!" shouted Kristy, and we all jumped.

"Girls?" called a voice. "Everything all right up there?" It was Mrs Kishi.

"No problem, Mum!" Claudia called back. Then she looked at Kristy. "Would

74

you calm down? You're being ridiculous. I know this is serious, but just—calm down, all right?"

"All *right*."

Once again, we turned back to our books. I began to have trouble reading mine. "Claud, can we put the light on?" I asked. "It's getting awfully dark in here."

"Sure," replied Claudia. She flicked on a lamp and the overhead light, then glanced out the window. "Gosh," she said. "There's a storm coming. Look at the sky."

Mallory, Jessi, Dawn, and I joined Claudia at the window. (Kristy remained planted in her chair.) We gazed out at the gathering clouds. A few seconds later we heard the low rumble of thunder.

"Ooh, creepy," said Mallory.

We returned to the books before Kristy had to waste any more energy on her glares.

"Here's something," said Dawn. "Well, it *might* be something." (A clap of thunder sounded.) "I hope that wasn't a warning," she added, looking toward the sky. "Anyway, this spell doesn't exactly counter-act bad luck, but it's supposed to get rid of it."

"Let's hear it," said Kristy.

"Okay. 'On a piece of paper, write your name, your birth date, your zodiac sign, and your lucky number.'"

"So far, so good," said Kristy.

" 'Place the paper in an airtight glass

container by an elm tree on the night of a full moon.'"

"We could do that!" said Kristy excitedly.

" 'The next morning, open the jar, add two hairs from an ox's tail, scrapings from the underside of a sea snake—'"

"Are you making this up?" I demanded to know.

"Unfortunately not," Dawn answered. She sighed and turned the page.

A streak of lightening cut through the sky outside Claudia's window. Inside, the lights flickered. I could tell we were all getting spooked. But we were more afraid of Kristy, so we kept on reading.

Half an hour went by. Nobody found a single spell—a single spell we could use, that is. Even Kristy was beginning to look bored and frustrated.

"Maybe we're going at this all wrong," I said, closing my book.

"What do you mean?" asked Jessi.

"Well, for one thing, we haven't figured out who sent the bad-luck charm. If we knew who did, maybe we could look up a spell to put on that person. A spell to visit bad luck upon the person. Something like that."

"Who says someone *sent* the charm?" asked Claudia. "It just appeared. That was part of your bad luck for throwing out the chain letter."

"But someone *had* to send it. I mean, it

76

came with the note and everything. The question is—who sent it and why?"

"Hmm," said Kristy. "I see what you mean. Like, is it someone we know? Or is it someone evil and unknown—an evil power-master, or maybe just an evil force?"

Jessi shivered. "Evil powermaster. You're scaring me, Kristy."

"Sorry."

"It *could* be something like that, though," said Claudia.

"Right," agreed Dawn. "I've read enough ghost stories to know."

CRASH! A huge clap of thunder sounded. Jessi and Mal screamed.

"Mary Anne, did you save the box the charm came in? Or the note that was with it?" asked Kristy.

I shook my head. "No way. I didn't want those things hanging around. Why?"

"They might have contained clues. I mean, clues to who sent the charm."

"Sorry," I said. "They're long gone. I threw them out the day I got the charm."

For a couple of minutes, no one spoke. We watched the storm and the flickering lights. Finally, Claudia said, "This reminds me of last Halloween."

"What does?" I asked.

"Almost everything. Remember all those thunderstorms we had last October? We don't usually have a lot of them in the fall, especially at the end of October. Plus, we

77

were solving another mystery then. The Phantom Phone Caller.

"Oh, yeah!" I said. "That's right. This is kind of weird."

"Who was the Phantom Phone Caller?" Jessi wanted to know.

"Well, it turned out to be Trevor Sandbourne, who had an immense crush on Claudia," I told her. Only we didn't know that at first."

"Trevor and I ended up going to the Halloween Hop," Claudia added. "Hey, did I tell you guys I'm going with Austin Bentley this year?"

"No!" we cried.

"Well, I am. But it's no big deal. I like him okay, but that's all." (Claudia used to have a crush on Austin. Bigger than the one Trevor had had on her.) "Who else is going?" she asked.

"Not me," said Jessi and Mal at the same time. (Their parents wouldn't let them.)

"Not me," said Kristy. "I'm tired of going places with Alan Gray. He's too much of a jerk."

"I'm going, even though no one's asked me," said Dawn. "I'll go alone. Who cares?"

"I guess you're going with Logan, aren't you?" Claudia asked me.

"Yup," I replied.

"Gosh, you are so lucky to have a steady boyfriend," said Dawn. "Someone you can count on."

78

"Even better that it's Logan," added Claudia. "Half the girls in our grade would kill to go out with him."

"Really?" I hadn't realized that. "Like who?"

"Like Grace Blume. Talk about immense crushes. I bet she hates you, Mary Anne. She probably hates our whole club for taking up so much of Logan's time."

Ordinarily I might have gloated about that, but what with the storm and the rest of our problems, I couldn't even work up a good gloat. The news about Grace just seemed like more bad luck.

10th
CHAPTER

Friday, October 30th.

Halloween Hop night! I couldn't believe it had finally arrived. It seemed like just a day or two ago that Logan and I were having trouble deciding whether to dress nicely for the dance or to dress in costume. But that was actually several weeks ago. Now the decision was long made, and I was in my bedroom putting on my costume and getting nervous.

Logan and I were going to the dance as cats. We had both seen the musical *Cats* and had been very impressed with the wild, furry cat costumes. We'd decided to make our own—a rough, tough tomcat costume for Logan, and a delicate kitten costume for me. They weren't nearly as good as the costumes in *Cats*, but they weren't bad either. Tigger crouched on my bed and watched me solemnly. I had modelled my costume on Tigger. I'd taken a black leotard and a pair of black tights and painted some grey tiger stripes on them, like Tigger's. I was wearing grey-striped gloves on my hands and (plain) black ballet slippers on my feet. I have to admit that Logan and I had cheated a little on one part of our costumes: we'd rented fur headdresses from a costume place in town. But we planned to make up our faces ourselves.

Now, seated before the mirror in my bedroom, wearing the leotard, the slippers, and of course the bad-luck charm, I painted black and grey stripes across my face. Then I put on the gloves and the wild fur headdress. I turned around.

"How do I look, Tigger?" I asked. "Just like you, huh?"

Tigger's eyes grew as wide as plates. He got to his feet and backed away, puffing up his tail. The fur over his spine bristled. He was a Halloween kitty.

I burst out laughing. "It's just me, Tigger, you old 'fraidy-cat."

I reached over to pat Tigger, but he sprang into the air and tumbled off the bed. Even though I felt a little sorry for him, I couldn't help laughing. I ran downstairs to show Dad the costume.

When I appeared in the living room, Dad glanced up from a book he was reading and jumped about five feet.

"Gracious, Mary Anne," he said. "That

is some costume. Especially that fur thing."

I smiled. "Thanks. Sorry I scared you, though. I scared Tigger, too."

"Why are you wearing that necklace?" asked Dad.

"This?" I replied, pointing to the charm. (I didn't touch it. I touched it as little as possible.)

"Yes. It takes away from the costume a little."

"Does it? I don't know. I—I just like it."

"Well, anyway, you are one amazing cat."

Ding-dong!

"That's Logan!" I cried. "He and his mum are here!"

"Have fun, Mary Anne," Dad called as I grabbed my coat from the cupboard. "Be home by ten o'clock—at the latest."

"Okay. Mr Bruno will drive us home. See you later."

I flung open the door and said hello to Logan, and we ran down the front walk to his car. We must have been a pretty funny sight, with our headdresses and all.

I tried to get a look at Logan in the moonlight, which was bright. The next night would be a full moon.

"Logan!" I exclaimed. "Your costume is fantastic!"

Logan had refused to wear tights and a leotard like me (I couldn't blame him), so he had bought a few yards of this cheap furry fabric at a sewing store (he had also refused to go into a sewing store by himself—I had to go with him), and he and his mother had made a fur suit for him. He was wearing a fur top, fur pants, and even fur-covered shoes. His hands and face were painted in tiger stripes like mine. And then, of course, he had put on the fur headpiece.

Mrs Bruno started laughing as we got into the car.

"What's so funny?" asked Logan. "The costumes?" He was a little sensitive about them.

"No," his mother replied. "You two look wonderful. It's just that I've never driven anywhere with cat-people in the backseat." (With her southern accent, what she actually said was, "No. You two look wunduhful. It's just that Ah've nevah driven anywhere with cat-people in the backseat.")

Logan and I laughed.

I was feeling fairly relaxed. Normally, dances make me incredibly nervous. They are not the perfect event for a shy person who isn't sure of herself. If you're happy with your hair, your clothes, your face, your body, and your personality, then you'll love a dance. But I'm never sure of anything about myself. The first time Logan and I went to a dance was a disaster. Now we've been to several together. Each one gets easier, but I still feel self-conscious. I always think everyone's looking at me. And considering I'm with Logan, maybe they are.

At least I didn't have to walk into that big roomful of people by myself. I hung onto Logan's arm as if it were a life preserver, the dance were a sinking ship, and I didn't know how to swim.

Nothing happened.

We just walked in. Everyone kept doing what they were doing, which was mostly eating. It always takes awhile for the dancing to start, even though that's what you're there for.

I looked around for Dawn and Claudia and Austin. I saw Dawn talking to a group of kids I didn't know very well. She wasn't wearing a costume, but she had smeared green make-up on her face and stuck a plastic wart on her nose. She looked like a young, blonde witch. I told you Dawn is an individual.

"Hi, Mary Anne! Hi, Logan!"

Logan and I turned around. There were Claudia and Austin. They were not in costume either, unless you'd consider Claudia's wild floral outfit, gigantic hair clip, and armload of silver bangle bracelets a costume. Most people would. Claudia didn't.

Austin, who was wearing a suit and tie, looked more like her father than her date.

"Hi, you guys!" said Logan.

I just smiled, suddenly feeling shy.

"Great costumes," Claudia said. "Who made up your faces?"

"We did them ourselves," Logan told her.

"Wow!"

Logan and Austin started talking about the JV football team, so Claudia took the opportunity to point out Grace and Cokie to me. They were dressed as punk rockers—really impressive costumes. Unfortunately, they caught us looking at them. Immediately they began whispering behind their hands.

"Those two make me so uncomfortable," I said to Claud.

"Oh, they just think they're better than everyone else."

"Really?" I replied. "That's funny. I always thought *they* thought *we* thought we were better than everyone else."

Claudia grinned. "Well, we are."

I grinned, too.

The band was really picking up by then, and more kids had started to dance. Claudia and Austin joined them. Logan knew it would be a *long* time before I would want to dance, so we wandered over to the refreshment table and loaded up on cakes and stuff.

"You know," I said to Logan, "this is better than dancing, but I do have to admit that it's a *little* embarrassing to know your English teacher is watching you stand around eating Mr Happy Face cookies."

"While you're wearing a fur head-thing," added Logan.

We finished eating. The band played two fast numbers, a slow number, and three more fast ones. When another slow one came on, Logan asked me if I wanted to dance. I could tell he was getting bored, so I said yes. Besides, a slow dance isn't really dancing. It's more like leaning in time to the music. I relaxed against Logan.

We danced and danced. It was an odd experience—dancing next to chickens and gorillas, space creatures and storybook characters, not to mention the usual hoboes and witches and goblins. Someone was even dressed as a stick of gum.

Except for one incident, I felt better about that dance than any other I'd been to. The one incident involved Cokie. She and the boy she was dancing with made their way over to Logan and me, and Cokie suggested switching partners. As we did (to my complete dismay), Cokie leaned over to me and said, "Cute costume. And nice bad luck charm. It really completes the outfit."

Okay, so Dad was right. The charm took away from the cat costume. I couldn't help that. And I couldn't explain to Cokie why I had to wear it. Only my closest friends knew the reason.

A year ago, a comment like that might have made me burst into tears and run home. But that night, I survived, simply waiting until Logan was my partner again. I didn't even tell him about Cokie's rude comment.

Then Logan and I danced the night away.

An hour and a half later, he and his father were dropping me off at my house. As their car backed down the driveway, horn honking, I ran to the porch, turned around, and waved.

I was just reaching for the doorknob, when I saw it: A note was taped to the door. My name was on the envelope—in those horrid, scary, cut-out letters.

My heart leaped into my mouth, but on the street, the Brunos were waiting to see that I got into the house okay, and in the living room, Dad was probably waiting to see if I'd got home in one piece. So I stuck the envelope in my jacket pocket, let myself inside, flicked the porch lights for Logan, and even had a talk with Dad.

I don't know how I managed to wait so long before I read the note, but I did. When I was at last alone (with Tigger) in my bedroom, I opened the envelope. The note was made of cut-out letters. This is what it said:

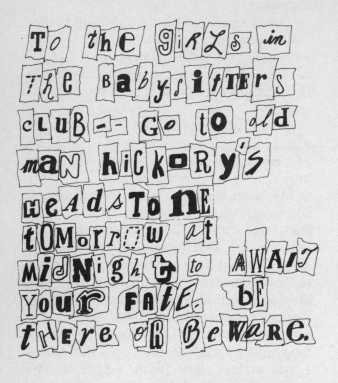

TO the girls in the Babysitters club -- go to old man hickory's headstone tomorrow at midnight to await your fate. Be there or Beware.

    I shuddered and held Tigger tight. Old Man Hickory's headstone was in Stoney-brook Cemetery. The next day was Halloween. And that night, Halloween night, the moon would be full.

11th CHAPTER

I spent an awful lot of time on the phone the next morning. My father may have relaxed most rules, but one still holds fast—no phone conversation can last longer than ten minutes. Well, that was a tough one. I had to call Kristy, Dawn, Claudia, Jessi, and Mallory to tell each of them about the note, and they had *millions* of questions. Each time I'd been on the phone for ten minutes, we'd have to hang up, and then my friend would have to call back.

I really don't know why Dad put up with that (except that he could see that *technically* I was following the phone rule), but I was glad he did. I'd hardly slept a wink the night before. I'd just lain in bed worrying. I jumped at so many harmless sounds and shadows that Tiger finally got fed up with me and mewed to be let out of the room. Then I was on my own for the rest of the long, spooky night.

I might have been relieved to see morning arrive—especially a Saturday morning—if it hadn't been *Halloween*. Since I was still a nervous wreck, I began calling my friends as early as I dared. That started all the phone calls back and forth. The thirteenth call was from Kristy.

"Hi," she said.

"Oops," I replied. "You know, you're the *thirteenth* call of the morning. That can't be good for you."

"Well, I'm not going to worry about it," Kristy told me. "And I'll put an end to the phone conversations. I am calling an emergency club meeting."

"*Another* one?" I replied. Emergency meetings are supposed to be rare.

"Yes. That note was for *all* the girls in our club, not just you. Well, anyway I think it was for all the regular members. Probably not Shannon. She doesn't come to meetings, anyway. But this is a group matter—a club matter—and it's serious. We're in this mess together, and we'll do something about it together. One-thirty this afternoon in Claudia's room."

"Aye, aye, sir," I said.

I wasn't sure whether Kristy would have thought it was funny that I saluted her.

One-thirty came around awfully slowly. After Kristy called the emergency meeting,

90

the phone stopped ringing. The morning crawled by. Dad didn't know what was wrong. He just thought I was bored and kept suggesting things to do. After I had filled a bowl with sweets for the trick-or-treaters, clipped Tigger's nails, changed the sheets on my bed, and polished some silver, it was lunchtime, thank goodness. Dad and I ate, and then . . . finally . . . I headed over to Claudia's.

I brought the note with me, envelope and all, in case it contained any clues.

Brother, if you thought Kristy was all business at any of the other meetings I've told you about, you should have seen her at Saturday's emergency meeting. I was surprised she wasn't wearing an army outfit or cracking a whip or something. If the graveyard business hadn't been so serious, I might (*might*) have laughed at her.

She was sitting ramrod straight in the director's chair. Her visor was pulled down over her eyes, and two pencils were stuck over her right ear. The club notebook was open in her lap. She was not talking to Claudia. She wasn't doing anything, not even chewing gum. As soon as I came in, she held one hand out for the letter, and gave me the notebook and one of the pencils with her other hand. In case I wanted to take notes, I guess.

Claudia and I glanced at each other, then nervously watched Kristy read the note.

Kristy let out a low whistle.

"Can I see it?" asked Claud.

Kristy handed it over.

Claudia turned pale as she read it.

Jessi was the next to arrive, and before she even read the note, I thought she was going to pass out from the mere sight of it.

Last to arrive were Dawn and Mallory (who live near each other). They took a look at the note, too, of course, and managed to remain calm, but I could tell they were scared.

All us club members could sense Kristy's nervous, businesslike mood, so when Dawn and Mallory had read the note and returned it to Kristy, we just sat in silence, waiting for Kristy to make the first move.

Kristy got right to the heart of the matter. "We've got to do this, you know," she said. "The six of us have to gather in the graveyard at Old Hickory's at midnight tonight, just like the note says."

"No way!" cried Dawn.

"Um, can I ask a question?" Jessi spoke up. "Who's Old Hickory?"

"Oh, he was this mean old man, James Hickman (his nickname was Old Hickory), who used to live in Stoneybrook," Dawn told her. "He was the richest man in town. Also the stingiest. Also a recluse."

"And what happened to him?"

"They just found him dead in his mansion one day. Some people say he died of old age.

Others say he died of meanness. Anyway, didn't want a big funeral or a gravestone or anything, but this long-lost nephew of his turned up, inherited Old Hickory's fortune, felt guilty, and had a gigantic headstone—"

"More like a statue," Claudia interrupted.

"— put up in the graveyard," Dawn continued. "Now it's supposed to be haunted by the ghost of Old Hickory, who's angry about the way he was buried. You know, that his nephew went against his wishes."

Silence.

Finally Jessi said, "And we're supposed to go to a haunted gravestone in a cemetery at midnight on Halloween—when there's a full moon?" She looked incredulous and scared to death.

"I think we better," said Kristy. "We all know what happens when we ignore warnings." She looked meaningfully at me. "Besides, I have a feeling something important is going to take place in the graveyard."

"Yeah, we're all going to die," said Claudia.

Kristy shot Claudia one of her glares. "That is *not* what I mean. I mean, I think there's going to be some sort of, um, confrontation. Everything will get cleared up. So we have to go. But we have to be together on this. We have to be a club, a team. If anyone *isn't* behind me, well, who knows what might happen. So—if you're

93

rk with me, to work together,
your hand. But you've got to

y raised her own hand to start things
wn was next. Then Claudia. Slowly,
ed my hand. And at last, Mal and Jessi
changed sidelong glances and raised their
hands.

"Great," said Kristy brusquely. "Thank you. Now, how are we all going sneak out of our houses tonight? I figure we should leave around eleven-thirty."

"Sneak out! Oh, my gosh!" I cried. "I wasn't thinking. I'll never be able to get out of my house at eleven-thirty at night."

"Yes, you will," Kristy told me. "We all will. Think. How could you do it?"

"I don't know. My father's the lightest sleeper in the world. Everything wakes him up. Look up 'Lightest Sleeper' in the *Guinness Book of World Records*. You'll find a picture of Dad."

My friends giggled.

"Well, I won't have a problem," said Dawn. "Mum could sleep through World War Three. All I have to do is walk downstairs and out the front door. She'll never know."

"I share a room!" wailed Mallory. "I'll *never* get out!"

"Don't you ever have to get up to go to the bathroom?" asked Kristy.

"Well, yes," replied Mal.

94

"So if Vanessa asks what you're doing, tell her you're going to the bathroom. She'll probably go right back to sleep."

"Okay . . ."

"I think *I'll* sneak out in stages," said Claudia thoughtfully. "I'll tiptoe to the bathroom, stay there for a while, tiptoe downstairs, stay in the kitchen for a while, then finally just leave."

"That might work," said Kristy. "What about you, Jessi?"

Jessi shook her head. "I don't know, but I'll have to be *real* careful. Mum and Dad had an alarm system put in the house. I'll have to find out how to turn it on and off. And how much time I have to get in and out of the house before I set it off."

Kristy began to look worried.

I knew how to shake her up a little more. "Hey!" I exclaimed. "I think I figured out a way to get out of my house. I just open the window, jump over to that tree branch, and climb down."

"Oh, no!" cried Mallory. "Didn't you ever see that movie *Pollyanna*? The one with Hayley Mills? She falls trying to sneak back into her house and nearly kills herself."

"Whoa," said Kristy. "Forget this idea. Just forget it. Alarm systems, climbing out of second-story windows. You guys were right. This won't work."

Really! I thought. Oh, good!

"I've got another idea," said Kristy.

Darn.

"I know how you can leave your houses pretty late—and *tell* your parents about it."

"How?" asked Claudia, Mal, Jessi, Dawn, and I. We were utterly mystified.

"Say that I'm having a late-night Halloween pyjama party, and that . . . that Charlie will be picking each of you up around ten-thirty and driving you to my house. Then he'll take us to the graveyard instead. Afterward, we really will spend the night at my house. We'll have a pyjama party there, to celebrate, after we've been to the graveyard."

"Celebrate what?" I asked.

"Not being dead," replied Claudia.

"Well, this sounds like a reasonable plan," said Dawn. "Except for one thing. What are we going to do between ten-thirty and midnight?"

Kristy frowned. "Oh, we'll ask Charlie to take us to Seven-Eleven for a snack or something. I'll tell my mum that's part of our party."

Darn. Why does Kristy always have to have such good ideas?

"And," Kristy went on, "Charlie will wait for us while we're in the graveyard. It can't hurt to have a getaway car . . . just in case. Later, he can drive us to my house. And believe me, Charlie can be trusted. He'll help us, and he'll keep the secret. Now do you guys think you can stick to this plan?"

96

I don't know why, but every last one of us nodded yes. It would have been so easy to say no and not go through with it. But now we were committed.

"Great. Then it's settled," said Kristy. "Charlie and I will pick you up starting around ten-thirty. Be sure to mention the party before then or your parents will never believe you. Then we'll go try to have some fun, and at five to twelve, Charlie will drop us off at the cemetery and wait in the car while we go to Old Hickory's."

"Lucky thing," muttered Claudia.

Kristy's last words before she adjourned the emergency meeting of the Babysitters Club were, *Tell no one about tonight.*

12th CHAPTER

Saturday - Halloween

There are some things you just never get tired of. Trick-or-treating is one of them. So when Mum and Watson asked me if I'd take Karen, Andrew, and David Michael around the neighborhood, of course I said yes. I hadn't gone trick-or-treating since I was eleven, and I kind of missed it.

Anyway, I'd forgotten that trick-or-treating can be a nerve-wracking experience for little kids. It's fun but... it's dark outside, people intend to scare you, and your mind is all cluttered up with thoughts of bats and cobwebs and goblins and who knows what else. So it shouldn't have come as any surprise that my little brother, stepbrother, and stepsister were pretty spooked....

Our emergency club meeting ended in the middle of Halloween afternoon. Kristy had agreed to take David Michael, Karen, and Andrew trick-or-treating at five o'clock. She knew they couldn't possibly stay out longer than an hour or two, so she'd have plenty of time to get ready for her spur-of-the-moment pyjama party before she and Charlie had to leave to pick us up.

What Kristy didn't mention in her notebook entry was that she was pretty spooked herself. Her mind was as cluttered as the kids'—only hers was cluttered with thoughts of midnight, full moons, haunted gravestones, cemeteries, and a town meanie nicknamed Old Hickory. While Karen and Andrew worried about rounding a corner and coming face-to-face with a gigantic Raggedy Anne doll or Snoopy dog, Kristy worried about mysterious spells, my weird bad-luck-charm, and who (or what) could possibly have summoned us to the Stoneybrook Cemetery at midnight.

She put her thoughts aside, though, as she helped her charges with their costumes.

"Andrew, are you sure you don't want to wear the mask?" she asked her stepbrother for the third time.

"No! No masks. I don't like them," Andrew said impatiently.

"But Andrew, it *makes* your costume."

"I don't care."

Andrew was going trick-or-treating as

Marvin, this cartoon moose he likes. Without his mask, he just looked like a kid in a brown animal suit. He didn't even have antlers. But Kristy could not convince him to put the mask on.

Karen was dressed as—what else?—a witch.

"Hey, Karen," said David Michael with a wicked grin, "aren't *you* going to put *your* mask on?"

"It *is* on," Karen said witheringly from behind her warty, grayish, pointy-nosed mask.

"Oh, I couldn't tell," said David Michael. He doubled over laughing. "Ha-ha-ha-ha-ha-ha."

"Come *on*, you guys," said Kristy.

"Come on? Where are we going?" asked David Michael innocently.

"*Nowhere*," said Kristy meaningfully, "if you don't settle down."

David Michael closed his mouth. He put his helmet on. He was dressed as a warrior from some Saturday morning adventure show.

"Ready?" Kristy asked the three trick-or-treaters.

Karen began jumping up and down with excitement. "Ready, ready, ready!"

"Buckets?" said Kristy.

Karen, Andrew, and David Michael held out their jack-o'-lantern sweet buckets.

"And I've got the torch," Kristy went on.

"Andrew, are you *sure* you don't want to wear your mask? You'd look a lot more like Marvin with it."

"Very sure," said Andrew, as the four of them started down the stairs to the first floor.

"Should I bring it with me anyway?"

"Nope." Andrew shook his head.

"Okay," said Kristy. Then she yelled toward the kitchen. "Mum! Watson! We're leaving now!"

She and the kids walked out the front door.

"Aughhh!" screamed Karen.

She had run into a ghost.

"Excuse me," the ghost apologized.

"That's okay," Kristy told him. "Don't worry about it. Karen, are you going to scream at every trick-or-treater you see?"

"No," replied Karen, sounding wounded. "Only the ones that surprise me. That ghost surprised me."

Kristy and her brothers and sister made it all the way to the end of the driveway before Andrew tripped over David Michael's homemade sword and fell to the ground.

"Aughhh!" he shrieked.

"Andrew, you're okay," said Kristy. She helped him to his feet, brushing him off.

"No, I'm not," wailed Andrew. "An invisible goblin tripped me."

"My *sword* tripped you," David Michael told him. "And you bent it."

"Oh. Sorry," Andrew replied. He stopped crying.

The kids walked across the street to the home of our associate club member Shannon Kilbourne. Darkness had fallen, and Kristy's little torch and the dim streetlight didn't shine away many of the shadows.

"This is so, so creepy," whispered Karen. She rang the Kilbournes' doorbell. She and her brothers held their buckets out and waited.

The door opened with a creak. A ghoulish face appeared.

"Aughhh!" screamed all three kids. Even Kristy (who'd been thinking about Old Hickory) was startled.

"Oh, I'm *sorry*," said Mrs Kilbourne's gentle voice. "I really didn't mean to frighten you." She lifted her mask.

Andrew glanced over his shoulder at Kristy as if to say, "See what trouble masks can cause?" Then he turned around again.

Mrs Kilbourne dropped a Mars bar into each bucket.

"Thank you," said the witch, the warrior, and Marvin.

The kids walked from house to house on the Kilbournes' side of the street. At every door, someone would drop something in their buckets. It was a sugar-feast that would have made Claudia proud.

At one house, a horrible-looking monster

was handing out nickels. Andrew was too afraid to take one.

At another house, a princess was handing out peanuts.

"Bor-ring," sang David Michael as they walked away.

They crossed the street. An hour later, their buckets were almost full, and they were standing in front of their own house again.

"There's just one house we've missed," said David Michael.

"Ours?" Karen replied. "You know what Daddy said. We don't get sweets at our own house."

"Not our house—Morbidda Destiny's."

"The *witch's*?" cried Karen. "No way. I'm not going to her house on Halloween."

"Yeah, no way," said Andrew.

"Hey, we've been over there before," David Michael pointed out. "For lemonade. Remember? And nobody died. Anyway, I'm not going to miss a single house on this street. If you're too afraid, then go on home."

Karen and Andrew looked pleadingly at Kristy.

"It's up to you guys," she told them. "If you want to go home, then run next door. I'll be along as soon as David Michael is finished at Mrs Porter's."

"'Fraidy-cats," David Michael whispered.

"Okay, we're coming," said Karen.

She and Andrew each gripped one of Kristy's hands. David Michael walked boldly in front of them. He marched up the front steps and rang Mrs Porter's bell.

Silence.

"Her house is kind of dark," Kristy said quietly. "Maybe she's isn't at home."

But just then, the door opened a crack.

Kristy gasped. She couldn't see anybody. But a low, eerie voice said, "Hold your buckets out."

Ever so slowly, David Michael, Karen, and Andrew edged their buckets toward the front door. Karen and Andrew never let go of Kristy's hands.

Plop, plop, plop. Something heavy was dropped into each bucket.

"Happy Halloween. Heh-heh-heh," cackled the voice. Then the door closed again.

Kristy shone her torch into the buckets as they hurried down Mrs Porter's steps. "What'd you get?" she asked.

"Apples!" cried the kids in dismay.

"Double bor-ring!" added David Michael.

Well, what do you know? thought Kristy. The witch hands out health food. She smiled to herself. Then her happy thoughts faded. She looked at her watch. Six-fifteen.

Six hours from then we would all be in the cemetery at Old Hickory's grave.

Kristy wasn't sure whether we'd be dead or alive.

13th CHAPTER

I'm not very good at hiding my feelings, or at covering up when something is wrong. This can be quite embarrassing. For instance, I blush a lot when I'm with Logan. And in school, if a teacher criticizes me or my work, I just might start to cry—in front of everybody.

So imagine how difficult it was for me on Halloween evening, trying to pretend that everything was fine—that there was no bad-luck spell and no bad-luck charm, and that in a few hours I wouldn't be hanging around a graveyard like a fool, with five other fools, all of whom could have been in their nice, cosy beds instead of waiting for the angry ghost of Old Hickory to appear.

It was next to impossible.

I was as nervous as Tigger. Every little sound made me jump. Any movement that I caught out of the corner of my eye made me

105

gasp. At dinner, I would have to tell Dad about Kristy's party—but I was sure there wouldn't really be a party that night. I was sure because I knew that my friends and I wouldn't leave the graveyard. Not alive, anyway.

I almost called Logan six different times. I wanted to tell him what was going on, but Kristy's last words at the emergency meeting had been, "*Tell no one about tonight.*" She had spoken as our chairman, and us club members always obey our chairman, at least where really important matters are concerned.

Even so, I knew what we were planning was risky, with or without Charlie and his getaway car. I've read enough Stephen King books to know that you don't go fooling around with the supernatural. And it was just a couple of weeks ago that Dawn had rented this movie called *Night of the Living Dead*, and we'd scared ourselves silly watching it on the Schafers' video. I certainly didn't want to meet any of those living dead in the Stoneybrook Cemetery. Not Old Hickory. Not anyone else.

Then there were all these awful horror movies that had been on TV the past week, and in honour of the actual Halloween, I'd seen *Halloween* and *Halloween II*.

I wouldn't have been a bit surprised if, when the six of us ventured into the graveyard and were looking around for Old

Hickory's tombstone, a clammy hand had reached out from the beyond and—

"Eeeeeiiii!" I screamed, sending Tigger flying. I was sitting in our living room, and a hand really *had* touched me on the shoulder.

"Mary Anne!" exclaimed my father. "What's got into you?"

"Oh . . . Oh, it's you, Dad."

Dad looked like he wanted to say, "Who did you expect?" Instead he said, "Dinnertime." Then he added, "It's just sandwiches. We'll be up and down during the meal, because of the trick-or-treaters."

I nodded. The reason I was sitting in the living room in the first place was because I was on trick-or-treat duty, answering the doorbell and dropping Milky Ways into waiting buckets and bags. It was only six-thirty, and already we'd given away 27 bars.

I followed Dad into the kitchen, trying to figure out how to tell him about Kristy's party. At last, I just blurted it out. As soon as we were sitting down, our sandwiches before us, I said in a rush, "Dad, Kristy's having a pyjama party tonight for the Babysitters Club. It's a late one so that we can, um, all help with the trick-or-treaters first. It was a last-minute idea, which is why I'm telling you now. Oh, by the way, you won't even have to drive me there. Charlie's coming over here to pick us all up. Around ten-thirty. Isn't that nice?"

"Splendid," Dad replied.

"Can I go?"

"*May* I go?" Dad corrected me.

"May I?"

"Of course."

"Oh. Thank you!"

The doorbell rang and I jumped a mile.

After that had happened four more times, Dad finally said, "Mary Anne, please. Tell me what's wrong. Is it Halloweeen jitters?"

"Um . . . yeah. Yeah, it is." That was a good excuse.

"Aren't you a little old for that? You know there aren't any ghoulies or ghosties, long-leggedy beasties, or things that go bump in the night, don't you?"

Well, I really wasn't too sure. So I didn't answer my father. Instead, I pulled the bad-luck charm out from under my sweater. I had made a decision. If my friends and I were done in by Old Hickory . . . or whatever . . . at the graveyard that night, I wanted Dad to have *some* idea of what had happened. I hadn't told Dad anything about my bad-luck mystery, but I wanted him to know, at least, that I had the charm.

"Dad?" I said. "Do you believe in bad luck?"

"Well, I—"

"Because a couple of weeks ago I was at that junk store downtown and I saw this necklace and thought it was really pretty. So I bought it. It only cost, um, a dollar-fifty," I lied. "Anyway, I've been wearing it ever since. But then this girl at school told me it's a bad-luck charm. So I'm really nervous. I've been wearing a bad-luck charm for days and days now."

"Why are you still wearing it?" Dad wanted to know.

Good question.

"I don't know. I guess now I'm afraid to take it off," I said lamely.

"Well, let me see it."

I stood up and walked around the table to Dad. He hadn't really taken a close look at the charm before then. I'd been wearing it under my clothes a lot. The Halloween costume was an exception. If I'd worn it under my leotard, it would have made a lump.

I leaned over, and the charm swung toward Dad.

He fingered it for a moment. Then a smile spread slowly across his face. "Well, I'll be," he said, looking rather fond. (Of the *charm*?)

"What?" I asked curiously.

"My grandmother used to have one of these. This isn't a bad-luck charm, Mary Anne. You know what's inside the glass? It's a mustard seed, which is a symbol of faith."

"*Really*? I—I guess my friend didn't know what she was talking about."

Dad and I cleaned up the kitchen then and continued to hand out Milky Ways.

While Dad listened to a jazz station on the radio, I did some thinking. Boy, did I do some thinking. First I thought of Cokie at the dance, and how she was just as big an idiot as the rest of us for believing that my mustard seed was a bad-luck charm. Then I realized that, since none of my friends ever speaks to Cokie, we hadn't *told* her it was a bad-luck charm. For that matter, we hadn't told anyone except Logan, who keeps secrets better than the Pentagon does. So why did Cokie call my necklace a bad-luck charm? How would she know . . . unless she had something to do with it? Suddenly, answers to the mystery began to fall into place as easily as the pieces to a jigsaw puzzle when only five empty spaces are left.

I remembered Grace's enormous crush on Logan, and that Cokie and Grace are best friends. All of a sudden, I was sure I knew who was behind the mystery of the charm, and maybe even why, although I still didn't know why my friends and I had been summoned to the graveyard.

"Dad, may I make a phone call?" I said. "I won't be long."

My father dried his hands on a dish towel. "Sure," he replied. "I'll answer the door-bell."

In the interest of privacy, I used the phone upstairs.

I dialled a familiar number. Karen Brewer answered the phone. "Hi, Karen," I said. "It's Mary Anne. Is Kristy there? This is important."

Kristy was on the phone in a flash. "Don't tell me you can't come tonight," she said.

"Oh, I can come all right. Now it's more important than ever that we get to the graveyard. Listen to what I found out: I showed the charm to my father, and it isn't a bad-luck charm at all."

"You mean it's a good-luck charm?" Kristy said incredulously.

"No. It isn't even a charm. And it doesn't have anything to do with luck." I told her what it was. "But you know what?" I went on. "Last night at the dance, Cokie saw the necklace and she called it a bad-luck charm. Now if it isn't really some symbol of bad luck that everyone knows about, and if we never told anybody that we thought it was a bad-luck charm, then why did Cokie call it one?"

"Unless . . ." said Kristy, catching on quickly.

"Right," I replied.

Kristy and I talked much longer than I had intended. That was because Kristy was in the middle of bad-mouthing Cokie and Grace, when suddenly she cried, "Oh! Oh! I'm not sure exactly what's going to go on in the graveyard tonight, but I do have an idea. We've got to talk to the others and tell them what you found out. More important, we

111

have to get to Old Hickory's long before midnight. Charlie can take us there right after he's picked everyone up. Listen, we'll need some things. Bring a mask with you. And a torch. Oh, and some string and a couple of white sheets and . . ."

Kristy was off and running with another of her famous ideas.

14th
CHAPTER

Just as planned, Charlie arrived at our house a little after ten-thirty. Kristy was with him, of course, and they had already picked up Jessi and Claudia. As soon as I got in the car, Kristy began making sure I'd brought along the things we'd need.

"Got everything?" she asked.

"I think so."

"Torch?"

"Check," I replied.

"Sheet?"

"Check."

"Mask?"

"Check."

"Great. And I've the tape player."

"I've got two torches, a mask, a sheet, and the string," added Claudia.

"Perfect," said Kristy. "We're really going to *get* 'em! . . . Are you scared?"

"Terrified," I admitted. "You?"

"Terrified, too. But there's nothing like a little revenge . . ." Kristy grinned wickedly. Charlie was keeping quiet. He must have thought we were all loony.

"Hey, you didn't tell Logan about this, did you?" Kristy asked suddenly.

"Not on your life. I don't think he'd have let us go to the cemetery without him. He'd want to come along and protect us. Worse, he might have tried to stop us. He might have phoned in an anonymous tip to our parents or something. Even so, not telling him wasn't easy. I tell him almost everything."

"Yeah," said Claudia wistfully. Then she snapped out of it. "Good for you," she said briskly. "I just hope the rest of us can keep this secret. Some of us have pretty big mouths."

We all knew Claudia meant Kristy. Even in the dark, I could see Kristy stick her tongue out at Claudia. But I didn't think Kristy would blow *this*. It was her idea. Too much was at stake. Could Charlie be trusted, though? I sort of wished we hadn't let an outsider in on our plan. Even an outsider with a car.

We stopped at the Schafers' and the Pikes' and picked up Dawn and Mallory. Then we headed for . . . the graveyard.

"Um, excuse me," Mal spoke up at one point, "but I have a problem."

Inwardly, I groaned. We didn't need any

114

problems. "What is it?" I whispered.

"Well, my brothers and sisters and I always hold our breaths when we go by graveyards. I'm not positive about this, but I think it's so that we won't breathe in any souls of dead people and get possessed. Once when we were out with our father, he parked the car in front of a graveyard while he mailed a letter. We all nearly turned blue. But now we're going to be *in* a graveyard for at least an hour. And I can't hold my breath for more than a couple of minutes."

Everyone tried not to laugh, although Charlie wasn't very successful.

"Mal, I understand that you're worried," I told her, "but I have gone by graveyards a million times and never held my breath. I've walked around *in* graveyards and never held my breath. And to my knowledge, no soul has ever possessed me."

"I've never held my breath, either," said Dawn and Claudia.

"I used to," Jessi admitted. "But when I stopped, nothing happened. Nothing happened when I stopped saying 'Rabbit, rabbit,' on the first day of a new month, either. I don't think you need to worry, Mal."

"Right. Worry about this," said Dawn. "We've just reached the graveyard."

"Pull up over there," Kristy commanded Charlie, "and wait for us. Remember everything I told you. Be prepared to go for help, okay?"

"You girls are crazy," was Charlie's only reply.

"Now, said Kristy, facing the rest of us like our gym teacher. "On to Old Hickory's."

Kristy wanted us to march to the tombstone in a line, but nobody wanted to be either first or last, so we went in a huddle. We tiptoed through the silent, moonlit cemetery, passing stark white tombs and every now and then a bunch of flowers or a wreath of greenery.

"Here it is," I said after we'd walked halfway across the cemetery.

"Here?" squeaked Jessi. "In all these trees? It's pitch black! Why are there trees here?"

"Old Hickory's nephew planted them. More stuff his uncle didn't want, but he went ahead and put them in anyway," Claudia said.

"Okay. Enough talk. Get to work, you guys," ordered Kristy. "We better rig up the ghosts first."

It was surprisingly easy. We stretched a length of twine from the top of Old Hickory's tomb to a tree branch not far away. Claudia and I had each sewn a curtain ring to the middle of the sheets we'd brought along. We attached the ring of one sheet to the tree-end of the twine and left the "ghost" up in the tree. We hung the other "ghost" from a branch of a second tree in the clearing.

116

Altogether, the six of us had six rubber masks, seven torches, and Kristy's tape player, not to mention the ghosts. Kristy played us a sample of her Haunted House sound- effects tape. My hair nearly stood on end.

Kristy was just rewinding the tape when Dawn said, "SHH! I heard something."

We stood stock-still, listening.

Not a sound.

Kristy checked her watch. "It's eleven twenty-five," she whispered. "Even if that sound wasn't them, we should probably get to our posts. I bet they'll be along any minute now."

"Our posts?" Mal repeated.

"Yeah. This is very important. Listen." Kristy gave out a bunch of orders. When she had finished, we scattered. I put on my mask, grabbed my torch and hid behind Old Hickory's tombstone with the tape player.

I was squashed up against the grave—on Halloween, near midnight, under a full moon. I had just proved something. Charlie was right. We really were crazy.

Kristy, also wearing a mask, climbed the tree to the ghost that was attached to the twine. Claudia handed a torch to her.

Dawn hid with the other ghost, holding her torch and wearing a mask.

Claudia, in charge of lighting, hid behind

117

another tree. She was holding two torches and wearing a mask.

Jessi and Mal crouched beside other tombstones, each wearing a mask, each carrying a light.

Then we waited.

We waited and waited and waited. It seemed like forever. When I dared to flick on my light long enough to read my watch, I saw that it was only 11.32.

That was when we heard the voices.

None of us said a word. We didn't have to. We knew what we were supposed to do.

The voices came closer. They grew louder. Just as I had suspected, they belonged to Cokie, Grace, and maybe three or four of their friends.

We didn't wait much longer. Up in the tree, Kristy let out a low whistle. It sounded like a bird call. That was our signal. (The other girls never even noticed it.)

I turned on the tape player—full blast.

Claudia began shining her torches around in weird patterns.

Kristy shone *her* light on the ghost in the tree and let him loose. He glided right down to Old Hickory's tombstone, where I caught him.

"Aughh! Aughh!" shrieked Grace.

"Help!" Cokie screamed.

But we weren't finished.

Dawn turned her light onto the second ghost, the one hanging from the other tree, and Jessi and Mal stepped from behind the graves, each holding her mask in front of her face with the torch lighting it up from behind. It was a pretty horrible spectacle— even for me, and I knew about the "special effects."

One of Cokie's friends was standing as still as a corpse and crying softly, "Oh help, oh help, oh help," over and over again. The others looked like they were getting ready to run away.

"Now!" ordered Kristy.

She jumped out of the tree, and the six of us surrounded Cokie and Grace and the others. We were all holding flashlit masks before our faces. Really—I'm surprised nobody had a heart attack.

The next few moments were pure panic and confusion. The other girls tried to run away, but we wouldn't let them. At last we put down our masks. The girls got a look at us.

"*You!*" exclaimed Cokie, taking everything in. "You little sneaks!"

"Us? Sneaks?" said Kristy innocently. "Look at you guys."

For the first time I noticed that Cokie's crowd wasn't empty-handed. They were also carrying sheets and masks and stuff.

"Is this what was supposed to happen?" spoke up a new voice. It was a male voice.

"Charlie!" Kristy shouted angrily. "I told you to stay in the car!"

But it wasn't Charlie who stepped into the clearing. It was Logan.

I was thoroughly confused.

"Logan?" I asked incredulously.

"Mary Anne?" he replied, just as incredulously.

"Somebody better explain what's going on here," said Dawn.

"Well, it won't be me," said Cokie, smirking.

"Or me," said Grace and the others.

"Then I'll talk," Logan cut in. (Cokie groaned.) "I was eating this nice, pleasant dinner tonight," he began, "when the phone rang. This voice told me to go to some grave in the cemetery at midnight tonight if I wanted to see something really amazing. Well, I'm curious and I like a little adventure, so I decided to go. Only I left early because I had no idea where the grave—Ol' Hiccup's or something—was. But when I got to the cemetery, who did I see, but Charlie Thomas, and he directed me to the grave, and I found my good friends" (Logan sauntered over to me and put his arm across my shoulder) "scaring the pants off *these* guys. Boy, are you cowards," he said to Cokie and Grace.

Grace looked absolutely crestfallen.

But not Cokie. "Talk about cowards," she said, "your girlfriend here was scared to death of the necklace we sent her, just because we said it was a bad-luck charm."

"So you *did* send it!" I exclaimed. "The chain letter, too?"

"What chain letter?" Cokie replied. She looked blank. I knew that the girls really *hadn't* sent it.

"But why?" asked Claudia. "Why did you send Mary Anne the charm and ask us to come here tonight?"

"Why do you think?" snapped Cokie.

"Believe me, if we had the vaguest idea," said Kristy, "not only wouldn't we be asking you, but we wouldn't be standing around in this graveyard in the middle of the night."

Cokie crossed her arms. Everything about her said, "I'm not talking."

But Grace spoke up. "Oh, we might as well tell them." (She said *them* as if she were referring to a swarm of flies.) "We just wanted to make you—all of you, but especially Mary Anne—look like, well, like jerks. We kind of wanted Logan to get fed up with you . . ." Grace's voice was fading away. It was hard to tell in the darkness, but I think she was blushing.

"Fed up?" Logan repeated, only he really said, "Fayud up?"

"Yeah." Grace kicked at a stone with the toe of her trainer. "You spend most of your time with Mary Anne and the girls in the Babysitters Club. There are other girls at Stoneybrook Middle School, you know."

"Of course I know," replied Logan. "I'm

not blind. And when I see anyone I like as much as Mary Anne and her friends, maybe I'll do something. But right now Mary Anne is—is my . . ."

Now Logan and I were blushing. I think he wanted to say *girlfriend*.

"Plus, I *like* babysitting," Logan finished up.

"So there," Kristy said to Cokie. She turned to the rest of us. "Come on. Let's go. Charlie's waiting." She turned back to Cokie and the others. "We'd offer you a ride," she said sweetly, "but the car's full. See you in school on Monday."

"Oh. Oh, you're not, um, going to tell anyone about this . . . are you?" asked one of Cokie's friends nervously.

"Who? *Us*?" I replied.

And Logan just said, "Maybe, maybe not," and smiled smugly.

Then my friends and I gathered up our equipment and walked off.

15th
CHAPTER

At Kristy's house later we laughed so hard that her mother had to come into her bedroom twice to ask us to quiet down. She wasn't mean about it or anything, but she did point out that there were seven other people plus a cat and a dog in the house who were trying to sleep.

However, in Kristy's room were six people who were so relieved they were nearly hysterical.

"It's over! My bad-luck mystery is over!" I said, after Mrs Brewer left for the second time. I tried to keep my voice down.

Kristy's room is gigantic. (Well, it *is* in a mansion. I hope I get to live in a mansion someday. Or at least in New York City.) Kristy's bed is gigantic, too. It's so big that four of us—Kristy, Jessi, Mal, and I—were sitting on it with room to spare. (That room was taken up by a large bowl of popcorn, an unsteady tray of drinks, and our masks.) On the floor, Claudia and Dawn were lying on top of some sleeping bags. (We hadn't even needed to bring our sleeping bags to Kristy's, since the Thomases and Brewers have eight altogether.)

Ever since we got back from the grave-yard we'd been giggling, eating, trying our masks on again (turning out the lamps, shining the torches behind the masks, and screaming), reliving the adventure in the graveyard, and talking about my mystery.

"I was so surprised when Logan showed up," said Dawn. "I know this is really awful, Mary Anne, and I'm sorry, but when I first saw him, I thought—just for a split second—that he was in on whatever Cokie and Grace were up to."

"Don't apologize," I told her. "That crossed my mind, too."

"Boy, we really got them!" cried Kristy, gloating. "We really scared them."

It was one-thirty, and not one of us was sleepy. We could only talk about the night and the mystery.

I took a handful of popcorn from the bowl. "You know," I said, "now that the mystery is over, I think I'll keep wearing the ch—I mean, the necklace. It really isn't a charm. And knowing that it's a symbol of faith, well, I don't know. I just like it. It reminds me of Logan and me. We're faithful. Especially Logan. He's been very faithful to me."

Jessi was frowning.

"What is it?" I asked her.

"Something's bothering me," she said slowly.

"What?"

"Something Cokie said in the cemetery. Only . . . I can't quite remember."

Jessi looked so serious that we all stopped to think.

"Do you remember what she was talking about?" Mal asked Jessi.

Jessi shook her head. "No, I just remember thinking that the mystery wasn't solved after all."

"Well, let's see," I said. "We know that Cokie and Grace sent the necklace. And they were going to try and scare us at Old Hickory's tonight, so they left the letter on my front door, too."

"Weren't Cokie and Grace both at the dance last night?" asked Dawn. "How could they have left the letter?"

"Well, then one of their friends must have done it. Anyway, they were behind it. And it was probably Cokie who phoned Logan tonight. What else is there?" I asked. "The mystery's solved. We don't even have to worry about spells and bad luck anymore."

"*That's* it!" exclaimed Jessi. "I knew something was wrong. It's the bad luck. The chain letter. Cokie said she didn't send it."

"I think she meant it, too. She looked confused," I added.

"And," Jessi continued, "the chain letter started the mystery. If Cokie and her friends didn't send it, who did?"

A hush fell over Kristy's room.

"A better question," I went on, "is— would Cokie and Grace have done what they did if I hadn't broken the chain?"

"Huh?" said Claudia.

"I mean," I said slowly, trying to think of how to explain my new fear, "maybe there *is* good and bad luck after all. Maybe Cokie and Grace were my bad luck. If I hadn't broken the chain, maybe they'd never have sent the necklace to me or tried to trick us or anything."

"Whoa," said Kristy under her breath.

"Remember?" said Dawn. "Our bad luck started as soon as Mary Anne threw away the chain letter—which was before Cokie and Grace sent the necklace."

Dawn and Claudia exchanged a frightened look. In an instant, they had moved the popcorn, masks, and soda to the floor, and squeezed onto Kristy's bed with the rest of us club members.

"I wonder how long bad luck lasts," said Mallory.

"Maybe we need a spell after all," I added. "Where are our library books?"

"I had to return them," Claudia replied. "They were overdue."

126

"Well, let's try to remember some of the spells," I said.

"Oh, please," said Kristy. "No. Not that again."

"We have to . . . don't we?" I asked.

"We do not," Kristy replied sharply. "Well, hey—we could make up our own spell."

"We could?" asked the rest of us.

"Sure, why not?"

"Because we don't know magic, that's why," said Mal.

"Oh, who cares? All we need is, like . . . Mary Anne, pull out one of your eyelashes for me—"

"No way!"

"Better yet," Kristy went on, "go get Boo-Boo. We'll take a sample of his fur."

Get *Boo-Boo*? I thought. Boo-Boo was crazy. I'd be taking my life in my hands. "Why don't I just go get scrapings from the underside of a sea-snake?"

My friends began to laugh. I put the popcorn back on the bed. The pyjama party felt more like a pyjama party again.

"You know," I said, "when you think about it, even if bad luck really was visited upon us when I threw out the letter, I think it's over now. I mean, those of us who went to the dance had fun. And we pulled a good trick on Grace and Cokie. Our luck is changing."

"I got an eighty-five on a maths test,"

said Claudia. "And Stacey straightened everything out with her father." Claudia pulled a make-up kit out of her overnight bag, and I began playing with her compact.

"I found my lost watch!" said Kristy with a grin.

"I don't have to get braces for six more months," Mal told us.

"My brother's getting A's in his new school in California," said Dawn.

"My ballet teacher told my parents I'm one of her best students ever," added Jessi.

"Then it's over," I told my friends. "No matter where the chain letter came from, just like I said before—the bad-luck mystery is over."

"We can stop being witches and go back to being baby-sitters," said Kristy.

I opened Claudia's compact. I closed it. It had a nice clasp.

Claudia handed me a jar of eye shadow. "Here. Try putting this on," she said.

I opened the compact again. And then—I dropped the jar of eye make-up. It landed on the compact.

It broke the mirror.

"Uh-oh," I said.

And Jessi, wide-eyed, added, "Oh, no, Mary Anne. You know what that means, don't you? Seven years of bad luck!"

"No! Really?" I cried, but I was laughing. "Well, I can take it. I've decided that since my mustard seed is a symbol of faith, we're protected . . . Because I have *faith* that we're protected. So, go ahead, you guys. Break all the mirrors you want!"

GREEN WATCH

GREEN WATCH is a new series of fast moving environmental thrillers, in which a group of young people battle against the odds to save the natural world from ruthless exploitation. All titles are printed on recycled paper.

BATTLE FOR THE BADGERS by Anthony Masters
Tim's world has been turned upside down. His dad's in prison, his mum's had a breakdown, and he's been sent to stay with his weird Uncle Seb. Seb and his two Kids, Flower and Brian, run Green Watch – a pressure group that supports green issues. At first Tim thinks they're a bunch of cranks – but soon he finds himself entangled in a fervent battle to save badgers from needless extermination . . .

SAD SONG OF THE WHALE by Anthony Masters
Tim leaps at the chance to join Green Watch on an anti-whaling expedition in the Falklands. However, events don't turn out quite as he expected. And soon, he and the other members of Green Watch, find themselves shipwrecked and fighting for their lives . . .

Look out for these forthcoming titles in the GREEN WATCH series:

Dolphin's Revenge by Anthony Masters
Monsters On The Beach by Anthony Masters

HIPPO BESTSELLERS

Indiana Jones And The Last Crusade (story book) by Anne Digby	£2.95
Marlene Marlow Investigates: The Great Christmas Pudding Mystery (fiction) by Roy Apps	£1.75
Marlene Marlow Investigates: The Missing Tapes Affair (fiction) by Roy Apps	£1.75
Swimming Club No 1: Splashdown (fiction) by Michael Hardcastle	£1.75
Swimming Club No 2: Jump In (fiction) by Michael Hardcastle	£1.75
Beware This House is Haunted (fiction) by Lance Salway	£1.95
The Plonkers Handbook (humour) by Charles Alverson	£1.95
Knock Knock Joke Book by Scoular Anderson	£1.95
Coping With Parents (humour) by Peter Corey	£1.95
Private Lives (non-fiction) by Melvyn Bagnall	£2.50
The Spooky Activity Book by Karen King	£2.25
Christmas Fun (activity) by Karen King	£2.25

Why not pick up one of the PRESS GANG books, and follow the adventures of the teenagers who work on the *Junior Gazette*? Based on the original TV series produced for Central Television.

Book 1: First Edition
As editor of the brand new *Junior Gazette*, and with five days to get the first edition on the street, the last thing Lynda needs is more problems. Then an American called Spike strolls into her newsroom and announces he's been made a member of the *Gazette* team too . . .

Book 2: Public Exposure
Lynda is delighted when the *Junior Gazette* wins a computer in a writing competition. But she can't help feeling that it was all a little too easy . . . Then articles for the *Gazette* start to appear mysteriously on the computer screen. Who is the mystery writer, and why won't he reveal his identity?

Book 3: Checkmate
It's midnight, and Lynda's got to put together a whole new edition of the *Junior Gazette* by morning. The only way she can do it is to lock the office, keeping her staff in and their parents out! Spike's supposed to be taking a glamorous new date to a party – how is he going to react to being locked in the newsroom for the night?

Book 4: The Date
It's going to be a big evening for Lynda – a cocktail party where she'll be introduced to lots of big names in the newspaper business. There's only one problem: who's going to be her date? The answer's obvious to most of the *Junior Gazette* team, but Lynda is determined that the last person she'll take to the party is Spike Thomson!

HIPPO CHEERLEADERS

Have you met the girls and boys from Tarenton High?
Follow the lives and loves of the six who form the school
Cheerleading team.

CHEERLEADERS NO 21:
PULLING TOGETHER Diane Hoh £1.50
CHEERLEADERS NO 22:
RIVALS Ann E Steinke £1.50
CHEERLEADERS NO 23:
PROVING IT Diane Hoh £1.50
CHEERLEADERS NO 24:
GOING STRONG Carol Ellis £1.50
CHEERLEADERS NO 25:
STEALING SECRETS Anne E Steinke £1.50
CHEERLEADERS SPECIAL NO 1:
(books 1–3 omnibus edition) £2.95
CHEERLEADERS SPECIAL NO 2:
(books 3–4 omnibus edition) £2.95
CHEERLEADERS SPECIAL NO 3:
(books 23–25 omnibus edition) £2.95

You'll find these and many more fun Hippo books at your local bookseller, or you can order them direct. Just send off to *Customer Services, Hippo Books, Westfield Road, Southam, Leamington Spa, Warwickshire CV33 0JH*, not forgetting to enclose a cheque or postal order for the price of the book(s) plus 30p for postage and packing.